A Love Worth the Fight

Thelma Magee

Contents

Prologue

Ray's POV

R "To the man who lives his job as his life and has been doing so for the last ten years, I salute you Ray!"

Tom Shaw, my best friend here at the air force base, raised his beer to toast me. Everyone else who was off duty raised their glasses and beers as they saluted my decade of service and I chuckled copying them and nodding my head in thanks before we all drank our alcohol. I thanked the many men and women who came up to me to congratulate me and smile gratefully when I was offered another beer.

"When the hell are you gonna find yourself a woman and give me god babies!?" Tom slurred. He had been drinking straight whiskey for the last two hours and only moved onto beer to help 'sober up' before he ended up dancing the hula like the last time he was off his face. I burst out in laughter and eyed him sceptically with one eyebrow raised.

"Who said I'd ever make you god father to any of my nonexistent kids?" I laughed slapping his back and watching him stumbled slightly under the force of my hand. I gulped another mouthful of dry beer and felt refreshed as the ice cold beverage slid down my throat. Even at midnight the humidity was enough to smother me and we were in air conditioning! I felt slightly bad for the newbie officers on duty but brushed it off... I'd been on duty for sixteen hours in the deadly heat and humidity during the day, this was nothing compared to that.

"As if you wouldn't make me god daddy!!! I'd shoot any bastard who tried to date your daughter and teach your son all my very best moves!" Tom shouted with a grin on his face as his bloodshot eyes were stretched wide in absolute seriousness.

"We'll see... I plan on serving in the air force for a long time bro, I don't really see kids in my near future. I'd most likely die before I find myself a woman understanding enough to be with me" I finished off my beer and realised that Tom was already gone to try his luck with one of the nurses.

I chuckled and shook my head at his short attention span and continued to enjoy my party. I grabbed another beer and walked over to the window that overlooked the ocean. I sighed in happiness that I was living my dream of following in my granddad's footsteps of being in the air force. I'd never actually met the man... but my mother always told me stories of how respected, determined, strong and dedicated he was.

She spoke of her father so mesmerizingly that I couldn't help, from the age of five, to want to join the air force as well. I finished my senior year of high school and immediately joined the air force when I turned eighteen. In no time at all I was a respected ground defence officer and never took crap from anyone. I wanted to end up being 'that guy' who was spoken about like my granddad was spoken about by my mother.

I shook my head in disappointment when I saw one of the younger officers on duty nodding off to sleep and knew that tomorrow every single one of the young officers I was training would hear about it. I believed that 'we were only as strong as our weakest link' and if something was to happen to the whole base because of one person... well, the newbies would soon be chanting that phrase in their sleep by the time I was through with them. I looked at the reflection in the window and saw Tom behind me with his lips locked on the nurse's and I checked my watch.

Half past midnight.

Well, he definitely works fast. My eyes caught my reflection and I took in my tall six foot ten height and my build that made me twice the width of the average man. Due to how tall and wide I was, coupled with my stern expression that I usually wore on duty, I was usually referred to as 'The Beast', which soon caught on and became a nick name of sorts around here.

My physical stature helped a lot when it came to my job and I loved every minute of the ten years I worked as ground defence officer. My job required a very high fitness standard and my fitness level was at the top of the charts so I applaud-ed as being perfect for the job.

"Congratulations Lieutenant Hodges" The General slapped my back with a wide grin. "Soon enough you'll be taking my place. Speaking of which... you're being spoken of to being promoted to Captain. Congrats in advance"

I smiled and felt pride well up inside me. I'd spent so long working my a$s off as First Lieutenant and I was finally getting the promotion I wanted. "Thank you, General" I nodded and saluted him respectfully as he turned to chat with the Lieutenant General.

I was moving forward and getting to places that I always dreamt of going!

Suddenly I felt the ground beneath me shake and in the corner of my eye through the window I saw dozens of men in black gear raid the base taking out the newbie that had nodded off to sleep with ease and without care. "We're under attack!" I boomed and immediately ran forward needing to defend my base and my trainees. All drinks were tossed aside as everyone sank into defence mode.

I only had my two Baretta M9s strapped to me so my first priority, after killing any threat to the base, was to reach the armoury and load up. "Beast! I've got your back!" I heard Tom shout from behind me.

I spared a glance to see my best friend with his standard gun out and looking as sober as though he'd never had anything to drink tonight and I nodded to him. I saw officers scrambling to keep the nurses hidden and safe as my team rushed to my side.

"Men!" I shouted to my team of both men, "I'll make this quick! Put down any threat to the ba$tards who thought they could come into our base and kill us off! Those with little or no weapons follow me to the armoury! Do not get killed!" A quick nod from them all and I turned towards the entrance and ran outside knowing my team had my back covered. I trusted my life in their hands as they trusted me with theirs.

As soon as I was out from the door, shouts and cries filled the air, second loudest only to the bangs and booms of the guns that were being shot from every direction. I had my eyes trained and focused on any man who wasn't in uniform and my arm was stretched in front of me ready to shoot with the intent to kill. A shrill cry came from my right and I ducked my head a little as I searched in the dark for the person it came from.

A female officer was beaten to the ground as a man in black hovered over her with a gun and smashed the handle against her temple before holding it directly at her face. Without any hesitation I squeezed the trigger of my gun and watched as the man's head cocked to the side roughly before he slumped to the ground dead.

I couldn't spare another glance at the woman as I moved forward, slightly crouched, and looking out for more threats. I had no idea where these men came from or what they wanted. I didn't recognise their clothing and couldn't see any of their faces so I wasn't able to see what they looked like either. The humidity was so thick in the air it was like trying to breathe through a pillow and sweat clung to every part of my skin.

I could feel the sweat trickling down from my forehead and also the back of my neck but I kept my mind focused at the task ahead of me. As I led another five men and two women behind me I shot off another few rounds, instantly killing the ten men hidden behind the line of jets. I tossed away my empty gun and took out my last one, hoping that I'd have enough shots left before reaching the armoury.

Explosions were being let off and I could feel the heat from the explosion from where I stood. "Watch for grenades men!" I shouted, hoping none would go off near us.

My hopes were squashed almost immediately when a grenade was thrown into the air towards us from far away. I saw the man who had thrown it and the many grenades strapped around his torso. I lifted my gun and shot him three times surrounding his heart and watched him collapse in a bloody heap. "Watch out!" someone called as the grenade began to fall down towards our group.

"Grenade!" I called out to them and jumped aside covering my face as I did so.

The explosion that followed soon after was so loud my eardrums wouldn't stop ringing. I hissed in pain when some metal shrapnel was thrown into my side and arm. I pulled out the large piece of metal that was hanging out from my flesh and threw it away to the side as the pain throbbed painfully. I couldn't hear a thing and my eyes blurred a little before focusing again. Tom was above me and holding a hand out to help pull me up. He was mouthing something, but I couldn't hear anything. Instead of the shouts, cries, explosions and gunshots that had just surrounded me, I could only hear a high pitched ringing. I pointed to my ear and shook my head signalling that my hearing was out.

He understood and pointed at the armoury... which was now on fire. Despite my hearing loss I shouted for every man possible to save whatever weapon they could. I followed after my team shooting round after round into the chest or head of the enemy.

I was about ten paces away from the armoury when a scorching pain I'd never felt before sliced through my thigh. I faltered just as another pain shot an inch down from the first pain. I stumbled and fell heavily to the ground as I realised I had been shot twice through the muscle in my thigh. My vision blurred a little at the pain and the tears that collected in my eyes didn't help either as I shot out rounds to make sure I wasn't going to be jumped by anyone.

The dead clicking told me I'd run out of bullets and I threw the gun away and grasped at my leg wincing and shouting in pain as my blood seeped through my pants and drenched the ground beneath me. My hearing began to come back slightly and I could hear Tom's familiar voice in the distance shouting my name.

"Beast!!! Watch out!!!" I heard him shout.

I looked towards my feet and saw a man completely covered in black raise his M16 rifle straight between my eyes. I was looking down the hollow barrel of his rifle when I quickly kicked upwards with my good leg and the shot rang out as his bullet soared into the black sky. As he was momentarily distracted I kicked at his knee cap and watched in horror as he collapsed onto my shot leg.

We both cried in pain but his were cut short as a stray bullet streamed through his chest splattering me with his blood and he fell backwards forcing a cry out of pain out of me again. The pain was too much. I was bleeding profusely and I knew that unless I was seen by a nurse or doctor right away I'd be dead. My vision became fuzzy and black spots dotted my eyesight before blackness completely took over.

I could only hope that my team wasn't going to die as well.

Chapter 1

Ray's POV

I stared blankly at the letter Tom had sent me as I sat in my hospital bed. I had read it over and over ever since waking up from my induced coma a week ago. After I passed out from blood loss our officers had been able to override the terrorists and suspected it was just a ploy to annihilate our base – a suicide shooting.

Tom wrote of how I was found, lying in a pool of my own blood, and rushed to a doctor at the base to see if I was even able to be saved seeing as my pulse was so weak. Somehow, by sheer miracle, my stats settled enough for me to be shipped back to my small hometown to recover fully. He told me that, after a 'suitable amount of time', if I wanted to rejoin the air force I would need to be examined to see if my fitness reached the standard required to do my original job.

A low growl slipped through my teeth as I thought of the last part. What the hell did a 'suitable amount of time' mean? How long was that supposed to be? What the hell was I supposed to do if I couldn't go back to being ground defence officer? I'd built my entire life around being in the air force. I lived, breathed and slept my job... and to find out I might not be able to do that... I couldn't even fathom what the hell I was supposed to.

I sighed and looked down at my left leg. Beneath the hospital gown and bandages I could just imagine the two circular scars that rendered me slightly disabled at the moment. Only one bullet had passed through completely, leaving another scar at the back of my thigh but the doctors had to search for the one that was stuck inside. The two bullets that were shot into my thigh had done pretty serious damage and as a result I was in terrible pain.

A short man with thinning brown hair sauntered into my hospital room and offered me kind smile. I stared back at him, not an ounce of emotion showing on my face. I was always in a bad mood since waking up. I was a big man and the hospital beds were barely wide enough to hold me, the food (though slightly better than at the base) was horrid and lacking any of the nutrients I needed and the ever constant pain in my leg overrode the pain all over my body.

"Dr Mitchell" I greeted him in a deep monotone voice.

"Good morning Lieutenant Hodges, how's the leg?" he asked me as he looked over my clipboard. I grunted and winced when I tried to shuffle back a little. "Still quite painful I see. I may have to up your dosage of painkillers" he mumbled.

He hummed a tuneless song as he went about checking my stats and the movement in my leg after checking how the rest of my wounds were healing. I had several stitches and soon-to-be scars all over my arms, legs and torso and my mind wondered to the saying my mother used to say to me whenever I developed a scar, 'It's just character building, sweetheart. Soon you'll look back and see how much you went through. Even if you were covered from head to toe in scars... it'll just mean you're a walking storybook'

I ghost of a smile lit the corners of my mouth before I put my frown back on. I sat patiently as Dr Mitchell finished up. "So what's the story Dr Mitchell?" I asked.

"Well, your stitches are all healing nicely along your torso, arms and right leg. The wound on your side from the metal shrapnel was infected but is healing quite well and shouldn't be anything to worry about now" He sighed and continued, "Now... about your left leg Lieutenant. As you are very well aware of, you were shot twice. The bullet that was stuck in your leg was lodged in your femur and had to be surgically removed.

"There was enough force, however, to fracture your femur, it quite was a big fracture but luckily not actually broken. The other bullet that did go through all the way had damaged the hamstring portion of your adductor magnus-"

"My what? Dr Mitchell... I'm no doctor or someone who's too familiar with clinical names of the anatomy... so please, for my sake... speak in English. Dumb it down a little for me" I interrupted Dr Mitchell. I was in no mood to listen to how much more doctors knew about how banged up I was and just wanted to know what the damage was so that I could work on fixing it.

"Of course. Sorry Lieutenant. Basically, the bullet went clean through and left a gaping hole that needed fixing up" he smiled at the bland way he explained it. "Both bullet wounds, including the fracture, will need a minimum of six months to heal then you have months of physical therapy after that to get back into the swing of things with your body" I nodded slowly and thought hard about what I'd just been told.

Months...

My recovery was going to takes months before I was even ready for physical therapy. What the hell was I going to do all that time?!

[Seychelles' POV]

I ran and dove into the water with my surfboard clutched in both my hands and felt the cool salty water splash against my tanned skin. I smiled as I paddled my way deeper into the water and just let my mind clear and let my body feel free as I sat up on my board with one leg on either side with water up to my knees.

This was my favourite part of my day.

Sitting in the sea, bobbing up and down with the light waves as I watched the sun say good morning to the beach. This was the only time I really got to myself and I always made sure I cherished it as though it was my last day. Ever since I was a little girl I'd always loved the beach. Anything to do with it I instantly loved, whether it was the sea, the sand, the sea creatures or the little colourful shells that I used to string into necklaces.

I breathed in a deep breath and smelt the salt as the wind blew lightly on my face. "Good morning world" I greeted no one in particular before leaning down again to paddle towards the bigger waves.

As the waves began to build I turned my board around back at the shore and paddled faster and faster before heaving myself up and standing with my knees slightly bent as I rode the swell of water. The wind whipped my hair back and the smooth glide of my board over the mass of water kept my bright smile on my face until I was out of the waves.

I walked into Shell's Gym, still smelling faintly like sea water even though I'd already showered and smiled at Naomi who was manning the reception desk. "Morning Mimi" I greeted her with a smile. She looked up and flicked her black fringe back from her face and greeted me back.

I walked into the gym that I was proud to call my own and silently congratulated myself on all the hard work that I'd gone through to finally pay off the mortgage of the building. No one understood why owning a gym would be a dream of mine, and I never told them the reason behind it.

It was barely past eight in the morning and yet there were the usual amounts of regulars that attended the gym, the majority of them running on the treadmills before they were off to their jobs. I loved my job as a personal trainer. I loved being able to help people reach their goals and become fitter and I gained plenty of clients because I made it my mission to make them feel comfortable as well as pushing them.

I was greeted by a few of the regulars who didn't have ear phones plugged into their ears and made my way to my office, which was really just a room outside the locker room big enough to fit a desk, filing cabinet, a few chairs and closet. I didn't really need to be in work until ten but I liked to take over some of the paper work from Naomi so I actually felt like I was running the gym, instead of just owning it.

I was thrilled to see that everyday there were more and more people wanting to join my gym instead of a rival gym and according to the little survey at the bottom of the contract for each client most were joining up because of good word from mouth advertisement. I did a little happy dance as best as I could while sitting down in my chair at the thought of clients telling their friends to join my gym.

"I'll see you later Mimi, I've got a few personal training sessions in the park throughout the day so I'll probably just catch you the next time you're working" I smiled as I left the gym with my duffel bag full of gear flung over my shoulder.

Even though I loved my gym, I preferred to have my PT sessions out in the park or by the beach with my client unless they asked otherwise. I threw my bag on the backseat as I hopped into the car and began to drive to Macintosh Park.

I worked through my five sessions and finally was able to go home. It was the time of day where there was just enough sunlight to illuminate the roads but the trees were darkened into silhouettes by the side of the gravel. I parked outside my run down beach house that was left to me in my father's will and walked inside practically dragging my bag behind me.

I tossed my bag to the side and flopped onto the sofa and listened to the low howl of the beach wind streaming through the little gaps in the side of the windows. My house had definitely seen better days.

It used to be painted an ocean blue and was sturdy as a house could really get, but it was old. It was originally built by my father's grandfather and passed down through the generations only to land with me and practically falling apart. Having concentrated on paying off my mortgage with the gym, I didn't have any spare cash lying around to have it fixed but I was hoping that that could change soon.

I was thankful that it wasn't raining today, Lord knows I couldn't be bothered setting up the eleven buckets up to catch the drips that passed through the ceiling. Even when it did rain, I no longer had to wait for the ceiling to start leaking to put the buckets down because I'd already memorized all the spots for every bucket to sit on.

It was pretty sad really...

My stomach growled and I groaned clenching my tummy through my baggy tank top. I forgot to buy food on the way home! I eventually hauled myself off the sofa and dragged my feet towards the fridge. I swung it open to look for something to eat and picked up a promising looking plate of leftover chicken. I sniffed it cautiously and grinned when it seemed fine. I heated it up and brought it over to the kitchen bench before digging into it like a starved lion.

After eating my bland dinner I took a long hot shower and fell into bed.

It was only nine o'clock but I felt exhausted. I really wasn't one of those people who could stay up for hours. I was a morning person and enjoyed the stretch of time in the morning where it was a cross between night and day and most people were still tucked in bed.

As I closed my eyes I let the sound of the waves crashing against the sand fill my ears. Who needed to watch TV or listen to music constantly when there was the sweet sound of nature just outside the door? The ocean always calmed and relaxed me and whenever I was away from the beach at night I could never sleep properly. I could feel my eyes becoming heavy and my brain became a little fuzzy as the sweet waves outside my window lulled me to sleep.

Chapter 2

I could practically feel my face turning red with the exertion I was putting myself through. Having spent years in the Air Force I didn't like to show the pain I was in, and instead preferred to work even harder. I had eventually been discharged from the hospital and was looking forward to finally getting out of the sterile building.

The bright sun felt amazing as it lightly sizzled against my skin and I heaved my large duffel bag over my shoulder as I hobbled down the path with my crutches to the closest cab. The driver nodded as I fell into the back seat and I felt the whole cab sink much lower under my weight. "Where to, Sir?" he the driver asked lazily as he started the engine.

I smiled softly to myself before fixing my stern expression back on and replied in my clipped commanding voice. He nodded again and slowly pulled out of his spot while I leaned back and closed my eyes, ignoring the throbbing pain in my thigh. Once the car began to move a little more steadily I opened my eyes and watched the scenery pass the window.

Home.

I hadn't been back in my hometown for ten years and it while it hadn't changed, it also had in a way. The small beach side town with a population of roughly three thousand people still housed the laid back and happy townspeople. Children laughed loudly while they played on the side of the street, or in cases of the teenagers on the street, while the adults watched from cafes or restaurants. The sun shone brightly with no traces of clouds and the black silhouettes of seagulls hovered in the sky before squawking and diving down for their meal.

What had changed were the buildings and shops that lined the street and the newly built houses that didn't look familiar. My eyebrows rose in interest at a new gym that seemed quite popular, if the amount of people inside had anything to say – Shell's Gym. Sounds... well, it suits the beach I guess. As we drove further I saw a few more gyms. I kept their names and location in the back of my mind for when I started my physiotherapy and was allowed to do more physical work.

I scoffed.

Allowed to do more physical work. The concept of not being allowed to do physical labour was such an alien feeling and I didn't like it one bit. I was used to hard, physical and almost bone-breaking labour that lying or sitting down like I'd been doing over the last few weeks was torture. I hated not moving around, using my hands to do something or at the very least being useful!

I caught sight of myself in the rear view mirror and took a moment to really look at myself. I'd lost some weight since leaving the base and was also a little paler. Despite the weight loss I was still much bigger than everyone at the hospital and noticed that they still gave me a wide berth whenever I was in the hallways. I rarely spoke when I was there, only speaking when I needed to and even then it was short sentences.

I was never rude, though. No, I was brought up well to be a gentleman by my mother. She always taught me to respect my elders, to be straight forward and honest. I was to be firm and strong-willed towards men yet respectful and gentlemanly towards women. Suffice to say, my mother was my hero and I didn't care what anyone else at the base had to say... I loved my mom and would carry the world on my shoulders for her.

Almost as though my thoughts had been preparing me, the cab stopped outside the familiar peach painted house with white framed windows and I felt a sense of welcome and ease overwhelm me. I thanked the driver and threw a couple of bills at him, offering him a generous tip before hauling myself out of the car with my crutches and duffel bag in hand.

I was home.

I shouldered my bag and crutched my way along the shell paved driveway towards the front door. I was excited and yet so nervous. Of course I'd always written my mother whenever I could and sent her money to help her out so she wouldn't have to work so hard but I hadn't seen her since I graduated and became a full pledged officer. She never visited me at the hospital simply because I never told her I was there. I didn't want to worry her and have her see me attached to machines and tubes. She didn't need to see that.

The familiar smell of home baked goods wafted over to me as I neared the front door and I couldn't stop the smile that grew. As always the door was open, no matter how many times I told her to keep it locked, and I walked inside dropping my bag to the ground just inside the doorway. Nothing had changed. Mom had kept everything just the way it was when I left and I loved how everything felt familiar. It was so good to be home!

"Katrina is that you?" I heard my mom call from the kitchen. "I'm just taking out the last batch of cookies for you"

I hobbled further inside towards the kitchen and leaned in the doorway watching my mom bend down to pull out the tray of cookies she was talking about. She looked as beautiful and wise as the day I left for the air force. Of course she had a few more wrinkles and was a little plumper around the waist but to me my mom would always be the most beautiful woman in the world.

"I'm not Katrina… but I wouldn't mind some of your famous cookies" I said with a smile tugging at the corner of my mouth. My mom gasped and spun around quickly holding her floral oven mitts to her mouth as her eyes grew to the size of my hands. I could see the recognition in her eyes (which were filling up with tears) but she seemed a little too shocked to say anything. "Hi mom"

"Ray!!! Oh my God my little Rayray is home!" she shrieked as she ran across the kitchen and enveloped me as best as she could in an embrace only a mother can give. "What happened to you?! When did you come back? How did you get here?

Why didn't you tell me you were back? How long are you staying for-"

I cut her rambling question with my burst of laughter and I squeezed her tightly back. "It's a long story. A few weeks ago. I was shipped back. You didn't need to see in hospital and at least a year according to the doctors"

Suddenly my mom smacked my arm and gave me a stern look, "And why did you think it was best that you kept this whole injury away from me? I am your mother! I am supposed to know these things!"

I knew she was only half 'angry' so I let myself chuckle at her angry Chihuahua face. If she had actually been seriously angry there was no way I would have laughed. In general, a child who respects their parent would be somewhat transported back to their childhood days when their mother got angry at them, especially when they use their full name. There was no way I was would step out of line if my mother had actually been angry.

"Because I was heavily sedated anyway mom, don't worry about it. You're the first person besides the doctors and nurses who've I've seen. See? You're still important!" She gave me one last stern look before smiling.

"Fine. But if this ever happens again, though hopefully not, you better tell me. I don't care how big and tall you get you are still my baby and I will slap you one on the side of the head if need be"

I laughed and shook my head at her motherly tendencies, "Yes, mom"

She beamed and I let her help me sit down at the dinner table while she prodded about every aspect of my life, not that there was anything else besides the Air Force. When I told her how I got injured and how I was shipped back she ended up crying and I immediately thought how much of a bad idea it was to tell her everything about it.

"My poor little boy" she sobbed.

"I'm not a little boy anymore mom. I'm fine. Just need a few months to heal and then a few more months of physio and I'll be back at the base like nothing happened" I told her, leaving out the part about the test I'd have to go through deciding whether or not I was physically able to return.

She sniffed the last of her tears and fanned her face lightly. "You will always be my little boy, Rayray. Now, get yourself settled in. Have a rest if you need it and I'll have dinner ready soon. I'll make your favourite!"

I stood up slowly and grinned. My favourite food was mom's lasagne. She literally had to make two of them because, even ten years ago, I would finish a whole lasagne to myself and sometimes even eat the leftovers of hers at midnight for a snack. She made the best food and I could already feel my stomach growling in anticipation!

I woke up in a sweat as I gasped for breath. My heart thundering against my ribs so hard that I held a hand to my chest for a while I waited for it to slow down. Every night... every night I had nightmares of the ambush on the base and the shots that pierced my flesh. Every night I'd been constantly reminded of how much it hurt to be shot, as though seeing the physical reminder wasn't enough.

I glanced over at the alarm clock and saw that the numbers read quarter to five. I wiped the sweat on my forehead and threw the sheets back. I wasn't going back to sleep. I'd feel even more tired and after ten years in the Air Force it wasn't too bad waking at this time. Normally I'd be up at five and that was a sleep in!

I grabbed my crutches and got dressed. My leg may need healing, but I needed to do more than just sitting around watching TV or doing nothing. I locked the front door and made my way down the shell drive way turning towards the hidden pathway that I found when I was younger. I wondered if anyone had found it during the decade I was gone and whether it was a common walk way now. It was a path that cut straight towards the beach with no need to travel around the trees, bushes and other roads.

To my surprise and happiness I discovered the path had overgrown with the thin spindly trees that grew by the sand off the main stone pathway and I grinned as I pushed my way through it. Obviously no one had found the hidden pathway and I felt like I was ten years old again as I pushed my way through the trees. The sandy path was still here, but the trees simply grew over making it almost impossible to see if you weren't looking for it.

As I walked, the trees thinned showing the sandy banks and other beach side plants. There were plants with thick leaves and bright flowers and little crabs that scuttled away before I neared them. I looked up to see the dark blue and purple sky with a faint dusting of clouds. The sun hadn't risen yet and the sand below my bare feet was cold and comforting. I knew that once the sun was in the sky the sand would be as hot as coals so I was thankful I'd brought a pair of flip flops.

I began to hear the soft crashing of waves and my smile grew. I'd always loved the beach, ever since I was younger the beach had always given me some sort of reprieve from the world. It calmed me down and, besides my mom, it was the one thing I missed the most while I was in the Air Force. I didn't see the beach much and I could really feel myself relaxing now that it was so close.

The trees seemed to close in again and I easily pushed through them sighing in happiness when the sight of endless ocean met my eyes. The sand surrounding me was a greyish yellow and the ocean was a dark grey blue. In the distance the first rays of light were beginning to streak themselves like paint on a black canvas. Where the rays of light hit the sky the sky turned from a dark blue to an interesting shade of imperial purple before lightening to lavender.

I walked slowly a little ways, leaving my crutches where the break in the trees were, letting the muscles in my leg work themselves a little harder as I walked in the sand. I'd heard it was better to walk on sand if someone had a leg injury because the muscles harder and I had to admit... that was very true. I'd walked for about ten minutes before stopping to sit on the sand bank. There was a lone surfer in the water. By the look of her bikini it was safe to say the surfer was a 'she'.

She sat on her board staring at the horizon and I turned my head in the same direction. The sun had begun its journey upwards and the top of the sun made its appearance over the flat line of the water. Sunlight burst out changing the sky all hues of colours. The grey-blue water lightened to a deep sapphire blue then continued lightening to a crystal blue as the water became shallower. The sand was no longer greyish yellow and instead it was easy to see that it wasn't a single colour, instead every shade of yellow, white and pink was on display as the sun rose.

I breathed in the air as a gust of salty wind blew in my face and I sunk my fingers and toes into the sand. I'd miss this. A lot. My life here seemed even more far away than the life I'd lived in the Air Force and it seemed odd that I could fit into both. I turned back to the lone surfer and watched in surprise at how good she was.

Her strokes through the water were so fluid it didn't look like she was even trying. I watched her as she caught wave after wave and I couldn't help but wonder who she was. Her body movements were so graceful and she had this sort of finesse that a lot of surfers couldn't seem to perfect.

Plus her body.

Wow.

Her body was insane, in a definite good way.

It was hard to keep my eyes off of her. In fact, I watched over for so long I didn't realise how time seemed to fly and too soon she was paddling her way back to the shore. She grabbed a towel that she had left in a pile with a bag and dried herself off before slipping on a pair of ripped denim short shorts over her bikini bottoms. She let her sandy blonde hair down and shook it out. I noticed it was longer than I'd thought reaching half way down her back before she wound it back up into a messy bun.

She grabbed her board and bag then flung her towel over her shoulder before walking up the sand banks and out of my sight. I sighed. Despite how much I loved the beach it wasn't the same as when I was watching her. I stood up and dusted the sand grains that clung to me and made my way back to my crutches. By now my leg ached painfully and when I finally saw the two metal crutches I felt relieved at having some sort of physical aid.

I walked back through the hidden pathway using the crutches and soon could feel the sand heating up beneath my feet. I slipped on my flip flops and continued walking. The whole walk back I couldn't help but think of the lone surfer. She didn't look familiar, though I was a fair distance from her to have a proper look. Was she new? Or just one of the people I didn't get to know before I left?

One thing I knew for certain was that it was going to take a lot to get her out of my mind.

Chapter 3

E very day I woke up at five in the morning, my body clock not being able to snap out of my early morning routine, and I'd walk through the same path and sit in the same spot to watch the same girl... just the same as every other morning since I first saw her.

I never tried to make contact, yet I never tried to hide the fact that I was sitting there and watching her. At the back of my mind I wondered if I seemed a little too much like a stalker, but in the end I just wanted to have my daily dose seeing this mystery woman.

It had been six months since I was injured and, according to the doctors, I was healing quickly and the morning walks on the beach really helped to strengthen my muscle. I had another appointment today with the same doctor to see whether I was allowed more physical work and I was desperate for him to say 'yes'!

The clouds above were murky and coloured with light and dark shades of grey. Colder winds whipped at my exposed face the water looked choppy as it rushed around in uneven waves. As always the mystery girl was out in the water, but I wondered why she even would be. It was obvious that the weather was far from ideal for surfing and she looked so small out there in the wide open ocean I was almost certain she'd get blown away by the winds alone.

I wore a hoodie over my shirt and shorts and I pulled the hood up to cover my head when rain began to shower down lightly. I was tempted to walk back home, seeing as the cold and rain always made my leg feel more stiff and sore but something told me to just make sure that the mystery girl would finish up safely. I wasn't sure if it was the 'officer' in me that told me to be protective of her (as I would with any other civilian) or just instinct that something might happen.

In any case, I listened to the small voice in my head.

The rain began to pour harder and soon I needed to squint through the haze of white downpour as I looked out for the woman who was still surfing... or trying to surf. The rain was cold and as it dropped onto the sand it left little dents as its souvenir. Over the choppy grey-blue water the waves looked angry at they all fought to crash down first and the rain splashing over the top didn't help.

For a moment I lost sight of the woman and stood up to see a little better. I searched side to side for her and relaxed a little when I caught her rise up from behind a crashing wave. "Come on... get out of the water" I whispered to myself as I stared at her stupidly paddle further out, "What the hell are you doing?!"

She turned her board around and began to paddle quickly as a gigantic wave swelled up behind her. I didn't notice I had stalked forward to the edge of the water, instead I kept my mind and eyes focused on the woman. The water rushed behind her and she pushed her arms, jumping up firmly on her board and riding the wave as it raged on. She stuck her hand out almost as if she was caressing the wave and then, without any reason that I could see from the shore, her board began to wobble and quickly flipped out from beneath her.

She collapsed into the water and disappeared as the wave as it crashed heavily over her with a loud roar. Her board, only visible because of how bright it was, spurted out the top of the wave and came sliding towards the shore as it rode the waves without its rider.

"Come on... where are you?" I nervously murmured into the howling winds.

Between waves I briefly spotted a flash of her bright yellow bikini before she slowly sunk back down and I didn't even think twice about ripping my hoodie off and diving into the freezing cold water. I bit back my gasp as the iciness bit at my skin and soaked my clothes immediately. The rain was warm compared the ocean water!

I kicked my legs and dug my arms out as I swam towards the last spot I saw the woman and hoped she didn't get washed out further too quickly. Waves crashed heavily over my head and I sucked in a deep breath before diving under to get further without nature trying to kill me too easily. A bobbing flash of bright yellow caught my attention to my left and I turned and kicked over to it.

I neared her and stretched out my hand as I grabbed hold of her wrist and yanked her to me. She was unconscious and facing down in the water so I kicked up to the surface and gasped sucking in beautiful cold air. I quickly pulled her face up but it was no use. The waves were violent and uncaring whether or not two solitary people needed to breathe.

I shouted out my frustration struggling to keep the both of us above water, which failed seventy percent of the time due to the waves, as I kicked with everything I had towards the shore. By now my shot leg was on fire despite the icy water and was beginning to seize up, but I refused to let both of us drown because of my leg. I pulled her up higher to get a better grip of her waist and swam harder and faster.

We were closer to the shore now and thankfully the waves weren't as tall anymore. As soon as my feet could touch the sand I stood up and threw her over my shoulder. With painful and shaky legs I carried her to the shore and carefully laid her down. I pressed my ear to her chest and realised she wasn't breathing.

The sky above cracked in half when a flash of lightening lit up the cloud followed immediately by a loud cap of thunder. The storm was directly over us and I needed to get her breathing before it got any worse. I leaned over her and performed CPR, thankful for my first aid training, and kept going until she began to cough and water spurted out from her throat. Buckets of water flew out and when she finally stopped throwing up water she collapsed back into unconsciousness.

"Sh!t!" I cursed loudly, only to have my curses swallowed by the thunder.

She was breathing, I could tell by the rise and fall of her chest but she was knocked out cold. A tinge of blood was oozing into her hairline and I had a feeling the reason why she was knocked unconscious was because she may have hit her head on her board. I needed to get her somewhere dry and I had no idea where she lived. I spotted my hoodie further down the beach and knew I had no choice but to bring her home. I scooped her up in a bridal hold and limped my way back to my hoodie. After grabbing it, which was much harder while carrying dead weight, I threw it over my shoulder and hers so that, even though it was soaked through, it was keeping the rain from pounding down on her face.

I wasn't able to grab my crutches so I groaned and limped past them as I made my through the short cut back to my house. With a throbbing, stiff leg and carrying an unconscious woman in my arms it took me twenty minutes to 'walk' back home. My mom was sitting on the undercover porch in her favourite chair when I burst through the bushes and immediately shot up tossing her book to the ground.

"Rayray! What happened?!" she cried in surprise.

"Open the door mom!!!" I practically shouted at her. Mixture of sweat and rain soaked my skin and my leg was almost useless to me at the moment as I dragged myself and the woman into the house. Mom directed me to lay her on the sofa and after depositing her safely on the sofa I collapsed onto the chair behind me.

"Rayray... what? How? I..." my mom stuttered looking between me and the woman.

"I'll be fine mom, just see if she's okay" I panted trying to make it seem as though I was just tired.

She gave me a worried look before nodding and turning to see to the little blonde surfer... the stupid beautiful surfer. As soon as she was no longer worrying about me I bit my lip muffling the sounds of my groaning. I clutched at my leg and took deep breaths as I tried to let the throbbing subside. It had been six months since the shooting, but with all the sudden weight coupled with the cold and rain... my leg wasn't handling it very well.

"She'll be okay Rayray. She had a nasty cut on her head but not big enough for stitches. She just needs to rest, I'll grab some of my old clothes. They should fit her and at least she'll be dry. You on the other hand... how's that leg?" she asked cocking her head to the side.

"I'll be fine mom. I'm just going to take a hot bath, will you be okay taking care of her?"

She nodded and gave me a small smile, "My baby boy, always a hero" She planted a kiss to the top of my head and scuttled off to find some dry clothes. I stood up slowly and winced at the stiffness in my leg before looking over at the little blond woman.

Now that we were closer and I wasn't scared she was about to die, I allowed myself to have a proper look at her. She was gorgeous. She had an amazing complexion, second only to completely airbrushed mannequins because of the cute sprinkle of freckles over her nose that one would only be able to see up close. Her blonde hair was tangled and messy but was pushed out from her face. Thick dark eyelashes brushed against her sharp cheekbones and her lips... Even though her lips were pale and slightly blue from the cold they were very, very tempting.

Her bottom lip jutted out and was a little plumper than her top lip. Perfect for nibbling. I shook my head and wondered where the hell cheesy descriptions like that came from. I knew I was always the romantic type, never sleeping with any woman who I wasn't dating, but I never usually thought or spoke like that.

"The cold and pain must be getting to me" I mumbled to myself before throwing a blanket over her goosebump covered body and limping over to the bathroom to sink into a hot tub of water.

I sat on the edge of the tub with my feet inside as I watched the hot water pour into the large tub. I was thankful that mom had forked out extra money ten years ago to install a larger bathtub because even then I was much bigger than other boys my age. I couldn't fit into the average one and now we had a spa-like tub sitting in the corner of the main bathroom.

Steam filled the bathroom fogging up the mirrors and creating a thin haze all around me. The air became a bit thicker and I breathed it in before stripping off my damp clothes and sinking into the soothing hot water.

I sighed as the heat immediately warmed my body and helped calm the stiffness in my leg. My shot leg felt as though it was lead and I massaged around the bullet wounds to help a little more. After my leg wasn't as stiff I sunk deeper in the water and let the rest of my body enjoy the heat. I pressed a button and the jet burst on and bubbles filled the tub. I shifted my position slightly and moaned when the jets pressed against my back. Now this was the way to relax!

Seychelle's POV

My body was wracked with shivers and my jaw soon began to chatter. Why was I so cold? Small hands rubbed my arms through some material and my eyes snapped open at the unfamiliar touch. "Who-who... who are y-you?" I chattered.

"Shh, don't worry sweety my name is Sandy Hodges. You hit your head while you were surfing and nearly drowned. I hope you don't mind but I put you in some of my older clothes. They may not be of today's fashion... but they fit you and are dry" Sandy had a kind smile and warm eyes that eased my nervousness and I sunk back down against the sofa.

"Thank you Mrs Hodges-"

"Sandy, please. There's no need for formalities here" she interrupted me. I smiled and continued.

"Sandy... Thank you so much. My name's Seychelles, or just Shell for short. I'm a little confused though. If I nearly drowned how did I end up here?"

Sandy stood up and I realised that she was quite short, nearly as short as I was and grabbed a mug, walking back to offer it to me, "Go ahead sweety, it's hot chocolate" I took the mug she offered and sipped at the rich and warm hot chocolate. It was delicious! Sandy sat back down in the sofa she was sitting in, "And as for you getting here, my son, Ray, brought you back. Nearly gave me a heart attack too! There I was sitting on the porch with my favourite book enjoying Mother Nature's rock'n'roll when out comes my little Rayray soaked to the bone, limping with an unconscious woman in his arms!"

I chuckled and raised my eyebrow, "Mother Nature's rock'n'roll?"

"Yes sweety, the thunder and lightning from the storm" she grinned.

I laughed lightly and sipped again at the hot chocolate holding it with two hands to let it warm my hands as well. "So your son, Ray was it? Is he still around here? I would really love to thank him for saving my life"

She smiled warmly at me and nodded, "Yes. He was going to take a bath and I suppose he'd be out to check on you afterwards. My little Rayray is very sweet that way"

Sandy's son, 'little Rayray' as she seemed to like to call him sounded like a nice young man. If she was his mother then I'd guess that he was as sweet as her as well. I sat up and noticed the sofa was a little damp. I frowned and realised it must have been because of me. "Oh no, I'm so sorry Sandy! I've made your sofa all wet now"

"Oh no sweety, it's alright. A life is more important than any material thing"

"You're very kind sandy but please at least let me dry it off with some towels or something for you" I felt quite embarrassed for barging into this kind woman's home and then ruining her furniture.

"Oh no sweety, really-"

"Please Sandy, I insist. Just direct me to the spare towels and I'll dry it off as best as I can" Sandy just smiled and shook her head at me in amusement but rolling her eyes.

"Okay, okay... There's some spare white rags on the bottom of the closet in the hallway. It's the third door on the right side" she chuckled and sat back picking up a book and reading.

I smiled and stood up keeping the blanket around me and walked down the hallway counting down the doors. When I reached the third door I opened it and found the white rags she was talking about. I stood up the same time I heard the door behind me open and I felt a rush of warm air hit me. I figured it was 'little Rayray' Sandy had been talking about and I turned around to thank him for saving me.

Now... what I had expected wasn't what I saw.

From short Sandy Hodges, who dabbled on about her 'sweet little Rayray', I expected a teenage boy maybe a little taller than Sandy if not the same height. I may have been guilty at thinking her son was on the skinny side, maybe sporting a few freckles and thick curls the same rich brown colour as his mom.

When I turned around to thank 'little Rayray' I was met with a six foot ten man rippling with muscles and shaved head. Not a freckle was seen but instead a multitude of scars covered his chiselled body and I couldn't help my eyes from travelling down his half naked body to the towel that was tightly tied around his waist. He was, for lack of words, a beast of a man.

"Oh, I'm sorry for scaring you ma'am. Are you feeling okay?" he apologised with a tone that was much softer than I expected. I was still in mild shock and couldn't speak so I nodded instead. "That's... good"

I was still somewhat openly raking my eyes over his body when he cleared his throat awkwardly and shifted from one foot to the other. "Thank you, Ray, for saving my life" I managed to choke out and looked up to make eye contact with him.

He ducked his head and beneath his olive skin tone, who he definitely didn't inherit from his mom, I saw a faint blush stain his cheeks, "It was my pleasure ma'am" he mumbled.

"Seychelles" I corrected him, "Or Shell for short"

"Seychelles... that's a very beautiful name. Very unique" he commented. I looked him over in a new light. Ray was a huge man. A manly man at that. His muscles bulked at first sight and his scars told a hidden story that I found myself very interested in finding out so it was plain obvious the man had a badass persona going on. Yet he blushed at a simple comment and seemed to feel awkward standing in front of me in his half naked glory. Ray Hodges was a very interesting man.

"Um... I should probably get changed ma'am... uh Seychelles. If you want I can drop you off home or anywhere you need to go once I'm done?" he offered.

I nodded. Despite Sandy's warm welcome and Ray's addictive quality I needed to leave and I wanted to check on the gym. "Yes, please. I'd really appreciate that Ray" He smiled and I nodded. I noticed that when he genuinely smiled, he had the cutest set of dimples appear on either side of his smile.

Ray turned to walk further down the hall and my eyes widened at the large black and grey shaded tattoo that covered his entire back. An intricate Chinese dragon had been inked starting from the back of his neck and across his shoulders, twirling down until it hid under the waist of his towel. I'd always loved tattoos on guys but never really large artwork, and yet Ray managed to pull off the mysteriously gentle giant with battle scars, tattoos and dimples.

He was like where 'opposites' came to meet in the middle.

And, boy, did the middle look good.

Chapter 4

R ay's POV

I firmly closed my bedroom door and limped over to my bed. The hot bath had helped with the pain and stiffness in my shot leg but the coldness from the rain and the extra weight while carrying Seychelles seemed to have forced a throbbing pain in my leg that wouldn't leave.

Seychelles.

It was a very beautiful name, and suited her perfectly. I was surprised when I left the bathroom and saw her in the hallway. She looked so tiny, even while standing up, and when she looked at me with her deep emerald eyes I lost my breath a little. Despite my 'beast-like' exterior and commanding personality that came with being Lieutenant, I'd always been a romantic at heart and never understood the men who'd have a new woman between the sheets each night.

I groaned softly, wincing a little at the pain in my leg, as I stood from my bed to change into something warmer than a towel. I felt the slight warmth of a blush across my cheeks when I remembered the way Seychelle's eyes roamed over my wide chest stopping to only briefly look over my numerous scars. I threw on the closest clothes and ended up in jeans and a long sleeve grey t-shirt. I pulled on another hoodie and limped over to my door remembering that my crutches were probably half hidden in the sand back at the beach.

I was faced with either having to wait until the rain passed or walk through the trees again to pick them up. "Screw it" I mumbled to myself, "I'll just limp"

I entered the hallway and slowly made my way over to the lounge to see Seychelles dabbing the white rags on the sofa and my mom eyeing her with amusement. "You know sweetheart, you really don't need to-"

"No, no Sandy I feel horrible at barging into your beautiful home unannounced and destroying your furniture. The least I can do is try to dry it out" Seychelles argued back with a flushed face.

I chuckled and limped into the room, "Last I checked I carried you in because you were unconscious... It wasn't like you had a choice"

Seychelles gasped and fell backwards landing on her backside. My mom giggled behind her hand and I threw her an apologetic smile before holding my hand down to pull her up. She placed her dainty in mine and I noticed how my hand basically swallowed hers. I tugged my arm back and she flew up and crashed into my chest.

"Oh sorry!"

"Wow... you sure are strong Ray" she gushed the same time I apologised.

"Well aren't you two just adorable! Stuttering together like a couple of high school kids" My mom laughed... easily breaking the awkwardness. "Would you like to stay for dinner Shell?"

"Oh no, I couldn't Sandy. Besides, I needed to pop by somewhere to check on some things before going home"

My mom spent the next fifteen minutes trying to persuade Seychelles that it wouldn't be a bother having her stay but it seemed as though my mom's persuasive manner was finally matched by Seychelles'.

"Oh okay sweety, but you be sure to come back to visit alright! I'll make you cookies!" Mom gave in while squeezing Seychelles in a fierce hug. My mom had always been this way. Open minded and completely welcoming to anyone she meets; this was why her front door was always open, much to my chagrin.

Seychelles chuckled and nodded, though she looked a little uncomfortable. "Sure Sandy"

"Finally ready to go Seychelles?" I grinned. She gazed at my face a little longer than normal and blushed when her eyes made contact with mine before nodding.

"Yep, all good to go now"

I grabbed the keys to the car I bought when I passed my driving test years ago and limped over to the door, opening it and motioned for her to go through first. Her eyebrows rose in surprise momentarily and she waited for me to lock the door. As soon as we stepped outside the howling wind hit us like a hard slap to the face and without thinking I wrapped an arm around her and steered her towards the car. She was so small and the wind was so strong that in the back of my mind I thought she'd fly away.

"Are you okay, Ray?" She asked me once we made it into the car, "Your leg looks like it's really bothering you"

"It'll be fine. It's just the cold and rain making it a bit stiff and sore" I answered her as we pulled out of the driveway. "I have crutches, but I left them on the beach..."

She was silent for a little while and her eyes seemed to understand something "...because you were carrying me... Oh Ray I'm sorry! Just tell me where they are and I'll go grab them-"

"No, no, no I'm fine Seychelles. I promise" I flashed her a smile and my eyes were distracted by her mouth. She offered me a little smile but was unknowingly biting her bottom lip, dragging her teeth across it.

I cleared my throat and bought my attention back to the road. The rain still pounded heavily and splashed harshly against the glass of the windscreen and I turned the heater on since I could feel the coldness seeping into the car. The gloomy grey clouds hung low in the sky it was almost as though anyone could scoop it up in a jar as a souvenir.

"So... where did you need to go before going home?"
Seychelles' POV

I don't think he realised it, but Ray easily took up three quarters of the front of the car. In the small space I had I couldn't help the amount of pure masculine hormones invading my personal space. He seemed like such an enigma. I found myself becoming interested in wanting to know what his story was... where did he get those scars? Why was his personality the complete opposite from his looks? (though that could possibly be rude to ask) And what happened to make him limp?

"So... where did you need to go before going home?" he asked. His voice was deep enough that when he spoke I could feel the vibrations in my chest and I ignored the erratic beating my heart seemed to have taken up.

"Oh uh... my gym" I answered meekly.

He chuckled and looked at me with a confused face. Another look that seemed so adorable on him. "You want to go to the gym? Uh... I don't know if you've forgotten Seychelles but you nearly drowned earlier" he looked at me with a deadpanned face, "I'm sure you can skip exercising for today"

I giggled and shook my head, "No! I'm not going to a gym to exercise. I own a gym Ray, Shell's Gym. I just wanted to check on how they are... uh, if that's okay?"

His eyebrows shot up, "Shell's Gym? You own it? Wow... I was actually thinking of joining up once I get the green light from my doctor to do more physical activities"

I tried not to let my mind drift off to dirtier thoughts of what 'physical activities' could mean and instead concentrated on his reply. "Oh really! Well, how about this, you come down to the gym with me and I'll sign you up for free for however long you want. You did save my life after all... it's honestly the least that I could do, and it's not really that much"

His face lit up when he smiled and I found myself looking at the deep dimples that framed his mouth. Dimples were adorable, and his were the deepest ones I'd seen. "Yeah? I'd love that, but I don't mind paying, honestly"

"No Ray, let me sign you up for free. I really don't know what else I could do to repay you and a free membership really isn't that much" he chuckled and nodded his head and I felt relieved at being a least a little bit out of his debt.

He pulled into a parking space outside my gym and pulled off his hoodie before handing it to me. "Put it on, you'll get soaked" I was about to argue but he shook his head, "Just humour me Seychelles. My mom always taught me to put women first and the goosebumps on your arms tell me a different story to what you're about to say"

He gazed into my eyes and silently dared me to deny him but he was right. I was freezing, even with the heater on and I meekly pulled his hoodie on. "Thank you, again" I whispered. His hoodie practically swallowed me. It smelt like apples and pure male and was so warm I would be happy to roll myself into a ball and camp inside of it.

Huh... I thought. I'm starting to sound a little creepy.

We ran outside, well Ray limped, and only ended up half soaked by the time we barge through the doors. "Shell, hey!" Naomi greeted me in surprise, "I wasn't expecting you to drop in..." her words slurred off when her eyes slide over to the beast of a man next to me and her eyes widened.

"Friend of yours?" she asked in awe.

"Saviour of mine, more like it" I corrected her, "He saved my life today"

"What-!" she shrieked.

"Don't worry, I'm fine. He's fine. It's a long story and not something I want to get into now. You know, you should head home Mimi. It's a twenty-four gym anyway and members can get in with their own cards anyway. I'll pay you for our whole shift but you should get home before the rain gets worse" I interrupted her.

A few minutes later and she was gone, thanking me because today had been horribly slow. I told Ray to go ahead and take a look around while I checked up on some paperwork and I watched him as he walked around the gym. He looked at home among all the work out equipment.

His sheer size was either amazing genes or pure hard work, or both, and I couldn't help but appreciate the hard contours of his body. It seemed as though every other member had decided to forego coming to the gym today leaving the whole place empty and just as cold as outside.

"This place is great" Ray commented as he sat down on the end of the bench press.

"Glad you think so. I poured my life into paying this place off, and now I finally own it" I smiled sitting on the bench press next to him holding his membership papers. I held them out to him, "Here, you just need to answer the questions and sign at the bottom and I'll need some ID"

He passed me his driver's license and I went to the front desk to photocopy them while he finished with papers. I sat on Naomi's swivelling chair and let my mind drift off while I waited for Ray to finish up.

Ray had saved my life.

It was really starting to hit me that I could've died today. I had yet to ask him for more details but I was a little embarrassed by what he would've been thinking when I was surfing out in this horrible weather. I couldn't help it though. Surfing was a part of my life, it made me feel more connected to my dead parents and I'd never missed a day.

Outside the wind blew hard, finding the small gaps between the doors and windows and making a howling sound like a lone wolf. I smiled at the comparison, I felt like a lone wolf ever since my dad died and I'd been just fine. A little low on funds at times... but I was fine. I couldn't help wrap Ray's hoodie tighter around me and I breathed in its scent liking how the smell of apples tickled my nose. It was nothing like the warmth of when Ray wrapped his arm around me outside his house but it was comforting, like snuggling in a thick blanket.

"All done" I jumped when Ray's deep voice jerked me out of my reverie.

"Awesome" I grabbed his papers and filed them away and grinned, "Welcome to Shell's Gym"

Ray's POV

"I'm totally fine calling a cab Ray, you and your mom have done so much for me already I'm starting to feel like I'm taking advantage of your kindness" Seychelles argued.

I rolled my eyes and raised an eyebrow at her, "Don't make me throw you over my shoulder and carry you to the car. It's not like I'm doing anything else and my car is just outside anyway. Come on, I'll drop you home"

I was starting to wonder why she seemed so unused to people helping her out. She almost always tried to refuse my help even it was plainly obvious to see she needed it. Surely she had friends, family and even a boyfriend who helped her out. I felt a pang of possessiveness course through me, I hadn't thought that maybe she had a boyfriend. Not that it was my business anyway...

We made another wild dash to the car and were lucky when the rain had slowed down slightly. I drove slowly and we talked about platonic topics, like the weather and the gym, in between the directions she gave me to her house. I drove up a long driveway and found myself staring at a nearly run down house by the beach.

In the corner of my eye I could see Seychelles look proud of her home but embarrassed by the state of it. "It's been in my family for generations... We all loved the beach" she explained as though reading my thoughts.

"It looks homey, like it's been worn in with good use" I smiled, "Plus it has a great location and view" She smiled at so warmly that the car actually began to feel a bit too warm and I tore my eyes from her to clear my throat.

"Want a coffee?" she asked after I parked the car as close to the front of her house as I could.

I wasn't really feeling for a coffee, but I was feeling for more of her company. There was just some sort of addictive pull towards her that had me nodding my head and running up to her door with her in no time. She pushed the door open and cursed.

"Damnit! I forgot about the buckets" she mumbled.

I followed her inside and even I cursed as well. Her house was indeed comfy and warn in with use. It was neat and lightly decorated with multicoloured hues of shells and starfishes. What I didn't think was normal in her home was the several buckets overflowing with rainwater that dripped from the ceiling and was now flooding her floor.

"Sh*t!" She cursed again before running forward and grabbing the closest bucket to empty down the sink. I copied her and grabbed two buckets and emptied them out as well. We worked in silence and only when the eleventh bucket was emptied did she turn to me with a sheepish smile. "Sorry about that, you probably think I'm a mess with what's happened today"

I looked her up and down. Her sandy blonde hair had a few strands scattered around her face and her face was flushed from running around the house and she wore the cutest sheepish face I'd ever seen. Her emerald eyes stared back at me and she was biting her bottom lip again. I couldn't help the loud laugh that came bubbling out of my throat and it felt good to laugh so loudly.

"No Seychelles, I don't think you're a mess. I think I came at a time when you really needed some help. And I'm glad I could be the one to help you out, speaking of which... did you want some help mopping the rest of the water?" There was about an inch of water flooding the entire lounge, kitchen and dining rooms but Seychelles was already shaking her head.

"No thanks Ray... I'm used to this" She looked exhausted as she came back with a broom that had a rubber end instead of bristles. "I just sweep the water outside"

I couldn't help feel a little protective over her. I don't know what had gotten into me but I urged her towards the sofa "Go sit down, I got it" I told her before practically yanking the broom out of her hands and started sweeping the water out the sliding door that led outside.

She didn't seem to have it in her to fight back and she collapsed on the sofa. It actually felt good to work my arms again. I did the occasional lifting of groceries for my mom and then there was carrying Seychelles back from the beach but I was beginning to feel a little more like myself now that I was doing more physical work.

I finished sweeping the water out and I chuckled lightly when I saw Seychelles snoring lightly on the sofa. I grabbed the blanket that was laid out across the back of the sofa and spread it across her. There was a notepad and pen by the phone so I scribbled her a note and placed it on the coffee table for her to see.

In a matter of a few hours I'd seen her sleeping twice in one day and was struck again at how beautiful she was both awake and while sleeping. I leaned down and hesitated before lightly kissing her forehead. "Sleep tight, beautiful" I whispered before walking out of her house and gently closing the door to face the rain.

Chapter 5

Seychelles POV

The loud greedy squawks from the seagulls outside pulled me from my dreamless sleep. What time was it? From the weak rays of sunlight that warmed my shack-like house I guessed it was somewhere around six o'clock. I sat up quickly wanting to change into the closest bikini then head down for a morning surf when a sudden throbbing wracked my head.

"Erghh…!" I moaned as I cupped my lightly calloused hands to my head. "What the hell happened?" It was then that the myriad of memories flooded my brain of the events that passed yesterday.

The storm.

The surfboard cracking against my head.

Waking up in dry clothes in an unfamiliar house.

Sandy Hodges.

Ray.

…Ray…

The gentle, scarred, tattooed, blushing, muscled giant with dimples so deep my diaphragm would forget to work causing my momentary lapse in breathing.

I swivelled my aching head around looking for him. Would he have stayed the night? It was then I noticed the blanket that covered half my body and the note sitting on the coffee table. I picked it up and smiled as I read Ray's surprisingly neat handwriting.

Sleeping Beauty,

I didn't have the heart to wake you up after sweeping the water out. You had a very eventful day and I don't blame you for falling asleep… even if it did bruise my ego a little bit. Just kidding.

It was a pleasure meeting you Seychelles, and if you ever need help with anything at all don't hesitate to give me a call. I'll be there.

I hope I'm not out of line when I say that you look beautiful when you sleep.

Ray

PS. Your snoring is very cute.

My hand flew to my mouth. Oh God, he heard me snoring?! Did I snore? Maybe he was just joking… How embarrassing. In any case, I couldn't wipe the smile off my face. I traced my fingers over the letter and re-read the few short sentences.

Did he really think I was beautiful?

I shook my head and gingerly stood up and when I wasn't being attacked by the hammering of a thousand tiny hammers against my skull I walked to my bedroom to change into a bikini and grabbed my towel.

I pouted when I realised that the surf board I used yesterday hadn't been at Ray's house and I came to the conclusion that it was either broken or long gone. Instead of grabbing another surf board, I decided on just walking along the beach. My idiocy of actually going out in the water during yesterday's storm made me cringe and I made a mental note to thank Ray again for saving my life.

I rubbed my arms with my hands as I walked barefoot down the cool sandy banks to the beach. Goosebumps prickled up on my skin due to the colder weather this morning. Despite the coldness however, I enjoyed the weak rays of sunlight that barely warmed my skin.

The tide was low this morning and the water waved from far back only rushing forward to barely tickle my toes. The wet sand was littered with starfish that were left stranded by the water and as I walked along the water's edge I bent down and toss them, one by one, back into the cool water. The sky showed no hint of the storm that had passed; instead the sky was painted with rough streaks of white clouds.

One by one, I threw the starfish back with a light splash into the salty water until I spotted a big, dark figure in the distance on the sand bank. I smiled and made my way towards the beast of a man sitting on the sandy banks staring at the ocean.

Ray's POV

I glanced down at my watch for probably the hundredth time wondering why I was waiting to see a flash of blonde hair in the water as the owner rode the wave. Seychelles was probably still sleeping for all I knew after nearly dying yesterday.

Just the same as every morning I woke up covered in sweat from re-living the near fatal gunshots in my dreams and dressed to head down to the beach. My leg was much tighter and sore this morning than others and the fact that I had no crutches to aid me around made me wince as I hobbled down the hidden path to the beach.

I was so used to gazing out and seeing Seychelles paddling out deeper into the water before riding back on a wave as I sat on the soft sand. However, this morning I was greeted by a calm ocean void of anything except the hungry seagulls. I plopped down onto the sand and felt the tiny grains between my toe and under my feet while my mind began to wander.

It had been just over six months...

I'd received no word from Tom or anyone else at the base for six months, since the letter I'd read when I woke from hospital. I couldn't help but feel a little disappointed at the lack of communication from my best friend but there wasn't anything I could do. There'd been times when I sat at the table with a blank piece of paper staring straight back at me and my pen hovering over the sheet, but nothing came to mind on what I should say.

I'm healing well... How's the blistering heat over on your side of the world?

No, it didn't seem quite letter-worthy.

I had to admit that I missed the funny bastard. He was serious when he was on duty and any time I needed him but he could switch off like a light and transform into this lady-charming, joke-telling man when he was relaxing.

I pulled the sleeves of my jacket down when a chilly wind picked up. It broke my mind chatter and forced me to look back out to the empty ocean. I was half glad Seychelles decided against going out to surf again this morning, and yet the other half of me was disappointed I would miss out on seeing her twist her body back and forth as she steered her board over the glassy surface of the water.

"Mind if I join you?"

The sweet, delicate voice that I already seemed attuned to made my eyes snap up to Seychelles' emerald irises. She was wearing a loose knitted sweater that dropped down to show her sun kissed shoulder and well worn ripped denim shorts that were so short she might as well not have bothered wearing them. Her tangerine coloured bikini strap wrapped around her neck and on her lips she wore a shy smile.

An involuntary smile crept onto my lips before I scrambled to stand up, "I don't mind at all... Sleepy Beauty" I winked at her cheekily.

She laughed and rolled her eyes at me, "Please tell me you were joking when you mentioned my snoring"

I slipped off my jacket and laid it on the sand before motioning for her to sit on it. Only after she smiled and sat down did I sit down next to her and continuing, "Maybe, maybe not"

She rolled her eyes again but playfully shoved her shoulder against mine. Even through her thick jumper and my long sleeve shirt I could feel the warm tingles spread up my arm from just her touch. What the hell was that?

I peeked over at her but she was staring at the ocean while the wind flicked her hair across her face, seemingly lost in her thoughts. I was never really one to talk much and it felt good to be able to sit with her without needing to fill the silence with chatter. I'd only known her for a day and it already seemed as though we'd been good friends for years.

"Thank you" she whispered. It was so quiet it was almost lost to the wind. "For saving me, that is. I know I thanked you yesterday... but I just really can't thank you enough. You saved my life Ray. That kind of thing doesn't happen every day to people like us. So thank you"

She flashed me such a genuine and sincere smile that I couldn't return it. "Well, your life was definitely worth saving Seychelles. And you're welcome"

I rubbed at my leg again and stretched it out wincing a little at the throbbing over the gunshot wounds. "What happened to your leg, Ray?"

"I was shot" I answered simply. "Well, shot twice really"

From the corner of my eye I could see her surprised face and her mouth hang wide open. "What?! What do you mean you were shot? How? When?"

"It's a long story... but I'll give you a snippet" I sighed and rubbed at it again. "I'm a Lieutenant in the Air Force and was off duty when our base was attacked by an unidentified force. Apparently it was a suicidal mass shooting and there were many of us who were either not or barely armed. I was leading my team to the armoury when I was shot through the leg twice while my back was turned.

'It nearly killed me from the amount of blood I lost, but they managed to save me and I was shipped back home to recover and recuperate. At least until I'm physically and mentally able to return." I turned to look at her wide eyes, "The Air Force is my life. It's... strange not being active, but I guess it's about time I was forced onto a vacation. If you could call this a vacation. I hadn't seen my mom for about ten years"

Silence fell over us, with nothing but the crashing waves and whistling wind as music, as she let the information I gave her sink in. "Wow... So I was saved by a Lieutenant huh?" she smirked, "That's pretty sexy"

I ducked my head and blushed, cursing my easy embarrassment for compliments like those. I admired her for not questioning me more about the shooting and instead replied with a single sentence that cheered up the conversation, "Nah not really. I guess it's instilled in me to help and protect others"

I glanced down at my watch and sighed. "Have somewhere to be, Lieutenant?" she asked cocking her head slightly.

"Yeah, actually. I have an appointment with the doctor at the hospital, apparently this is where I may or may not be 'allowed' to do more rigorous work" I was actually kind of nervous. I was desperate to get the official 'yes' from the Doc so I could get back into shape and I hoped that yesterday didn't set me back. Not that I regretted it, not at all!

I heaved myself up and Seychelles copied me before dusting off my jacket and handing it to me. "Thanks" she nodded her head at my jacket, "Well, uh... I guess I'll see you around. Good luck with the appointment"

"Thanks Sleeping Beauty" I smirked. "Hopefully I'll bump into you soon"

With one last smile she turned around and walked back the way she came while I spun back to the pathway and collected my crutches on the way. I didn't want to tire myself out before I was tested.

I was ecstatic!

The doctor was more than happy with my progress and gave two thumbs up for me to get back to physical activities again and the first thing I wanted to do was put my free membership to the gym to good use. I was driving my old car back to my house whistling a tune that matched my happy mood. The sun was blazing brightly in the cerulean sky and birds sang brightly.

I cut the engine on the drive way and made my way to the front door when I suddenly stopped. Perhaps it was the airman in me, or maybe it was just instinct but I knew that someone else besides my mom was at home.

I silently walked over and, not surprisingly, the front door was open. The deep chuckle of a man came from the kitchen and I wondered who the mystery man could be. I was more than ready to knock the lights out of any man who would hurt my mom.

"These are, swear to all that is holy and unholy, the best cookies on the face of the planet Sandy" The man gushed through a mouthful of, apparently, cookies.

The voice was immediately familiar and a grin broke out onto my face. "Tom! What the hell are you doing here?" I called out as I walked around the corner.

Tom's raven black hair was longer than the last time I saw him but other than that he was exactly the same. The same chestnut brown eyes that crinkled slightly at the corners when he smiled and his laugh was still as boisterous as ever.

Tom turned to me and the next thing I know he'd jumped off the chair he was sitting on and ran over to tackle me to the ground. I groaned. "So the little man child has finally showed up! Good to see you Beast!" He laughed as he messed up my hair that had grown a little and stood up. "I was expecting you back already! What's taking you so long?!"

"Fu-freaking hell, Tom!" I corrected myself glancing over at my mom, "I'm still recovering! The doctor said it'd be a least a year and I only just got clearance from him to be able to do physical work"

"Rayray, that's fantastic news!" Mom squealed but Tom rolled his eyes at me.

"Clearance, smearance... it's a good thing I'm here then because the Beast I know would only ever follow orders from the higher ups. Looks like I'll need to give you a little push to get back onto track. You look like you gained a few inches around your waist there buddy" He patted my still flat stomach.

I knocked his hands away and rolled my eyes. "I was about to smart ass... I came back home to change so I could head over t the gym to get started again. I've missed it"

Tom nodded his head and sat back down on the chair, "Good. It's just not the same without the Beast on the prowl for weak links back at the base.

"Give me a minute to change then we'll both head over to the gym. I've already signed up to it.

"Well get going then! Time's a-wasting"

"The Beast is in the house!" Tom shouted as we entered the gym. A few men glanced our way before rolling their eyes and concentrating on their weights again while a few of the women present gave us an appreciative once over. "Yum, yum" he commented quietly at the ones running on the treadmill.

I felt back to my normal self as I huffed another breath out as I pushed the heavy weights up. Sweat trickled down my face and covered my skin from the effort it took. Tom and I had been at the gym for almost an hour already and he was acting more like an angry coach than a friend who 'wanted to give me that little extra push'.

"That's it Beast! Give me one more! Don't be such a girl!" he shouted from behind me.

"Beast, huh? That actually suits you quite well" A honey sweet voice commented from my side. That sexy voice could only be one woman. Seychelles.

She'd caught me off guard and I quickly looked over to her and lost concentration on the weights I was currently holding above me. Seychelles was wearing a black and yellow cropped top and a pair of tight black leggings with running shoes and her skin was slick with sweat. She was throwing me a half smirk and winked when she caught my eye. It was only of the sexiest sights I'd ever seen.

The weights swayed and tilted a little too far to my left. Before I could centre it above me again it quickly swung further and fell straight to the ground... taking me with it. I fell off the bench press with a heavy thud and ended up lying on the ground. I swiftly scrambled up to see if she saw that horrifyingly embarrassing moment.

Of course she did.

"Shit! That was my bad Beast!" Tom apologised.

"Ray are you okay?!" Seychelles called out running towards me.

"I'm fine, I'm fine" I quickly said, "It's just my dignity and pride that hurts a little. So what are you up to Sleeping Beauty" I smiled at her while I stood up.

Before she could answer Tom snorted with laughter. "Sleeping Beauty? Shouldn't her name be 'Beauty' if she's going to be affiliated with you? You are, after all, the Beast "

Chapter 6

R ay's POV

"Beauty" I twirled the new nick name around my tongue, "I like it… it's very suiting for you Seychelles" I winked at her.

Her face was already tinged pink from working out but I was sure that her face grew a little darker at the compliment and I felt a sense of pride at making the rose coloured tint flush against her flawless skin. In the corner of my eyes I could see Tom eye Seychelles up and down before he 'oh so subtly' elbowed me in the ribs.

I barely winced and instead rolled my eyes, "Tom this is Seychelles, Damsel in Distress, amazing surfer and owner of this gym" I chuckled as I winked at Seychelles again, "Beauty this is Tom. My best friend and the man who's got my back at the base"

The two shook hands and I immediately saw Tom turn on the charm as he stared straight into Seychelles eyes and held her hand for longer than necessary. He stroked his thumb over her hand briefly before letting go, "It's most definitely my pleasure, Seychelles"

She raised an eyebrow slightly but smiled, "Right back at you Tom"

Tom stepped forward, completely forgetting he was supposedly here to force me back into shape, and began to flirt with Seychelles like the world was about to end at any given moment. I shook my head and laid back down on the bench press getting back to my weights.

Tom was an uncontrollable flirt. A 'charmer' as the women back at the base put it. His chestnut brown hair had grown slightly out from the air force regulated hair cut and his light coffee coloured eyes were an odd shade which, according to him, 'made the women find him fascinating'. I frowned when I saw him lean towards Seychelles as he swiped away some invisible dirt off her shoulders.

When it came to the field, I knew how to kill it, I was top of the rank when it came to all things physical and no one could come close to matching my skill. But when it came to playing the field Tom knew all the moves. As soon as I found out he was with one woman, he was already onto the next. He never left them sullen though, but he was fast becoming known as the Cobra Player.

He strikes with lightening speed.

I turned my eyes from the flirting couple (though I realised Tom was doing almost all the talking) and instead concentrated on the black smudge on the ceiling as I pushed the heavy weights away from my chest over and over again. Sweat dripped from my naked torso and I could feel my body heating up more now that I was completely focused.

I hung the bar back and slid my hands towards the middle to work my triceps out. Tom's flirting had faded into the background and the only sound I could hear was the rushing blood in my ears and my heavy breathing. I took another breath before lifting it off and began my reps, pushing the weights up then down, then up and down again.

"You have great technique, Ray" Seychelles soft voice complimented me. My breathing hitched at her unexpected appearance but luckily I didn't drop the weights and fall off the bench press again. "But let me just fix you up here"

Seychelles was standing by my head and she leaned forward to place her hands over mine as she slid them a little closer together. She was leaning so low. I wasn't sure if the air conditioning had stopped working because it was suddenly very, very hot. My eyes roamed away from our touching hands to watch the bead of sweat that rolled leisurely down her throat and drip slowly down into the valley of her brea$ts.

"-will work your triceps a lot better this way"

I shook my head and coughed when I realised I'd been staring at her chest for who knows how long. This was odd... I was usually more respectful than this. "Sorry, what?" I asked.

Seychelles lips parted and she smiled patiently at me, "I said if you move your hands slightly closer like this and make your reps slower it'll work your triceps a lot better this way. Make sure the bar can reach your chest but be sure to keep your elbows close to your sides, that's very important" I listened and instantly I felt the difference when I listened to her advice.

She leaned down again and held her hands under my elbows to keep them tight to my side as I brought the bar down leaving me way, way too close to her amazing body for comfort right now. I felt a certain stirring in my lower region and my eyes widened. Crap!

I moved my eyes back to the smudge on the ceiling and tried to think of other things to take my mind off the flawless, supple skin of her mounds that were damp with perspiration and hung dangerously close to my face... close enough to nuzzle my nose between her brea$ts and-

Stop it! Think of anything else!

Weights. Running. Physical exam. Air Force. Base. Heat... hot... hot flushed skin...sweat that rolled down between Seychelles'-

"I think I'm done!" I practically shouted as I pushed the bar back up and hooked it back on the stand. I rolled forward almost head butting Seychelles on my way up and stood up quickly grabbing my discarded t-shirt and holding it in front of my growing erect!on.

She looked a little surprised at my sudden change but smiled anyway and nodded as she stepped back. "Oh, okay sure" she replied a little breathlessly. I winked at her and practically ran to the locker room to throw myself into a cold shower.

I leaned my head against the cold, white tiles of the wall and heaved a heavy sigh. "What the hell was that?" I asked myself. When I was all finished I grabbed my bag and threw my towel around my shoulders.

My hair had grown longer and I was starting to get used to the feeling of my hair actually growing, instead of the shaved style I'd worn for years.As I stepped back into the gym I saw Seychelles standing with Tom and the man himself was leaning against the wall as he turned the charm back on. While I watched him interact with Seychelles I couldn't help the uncomfortable feeling in my chest; for the first time in knows how long I felt a little lost and inadequate.

Seychelles emerald eyes caught mine and the smile that curved onto her plump pink lips was enough to take away the unease I felt inside. "Looking fresh Ray" she winked.

I smiled back in reply. "Thanks for the help Beauty" Seychelles answered me with a blush and a roll of her eyes.

"So, how about I take you out sometime beautiful?" Tom asked bringing the attention back to him. Seychelles looked back at him but before she could reply I interrupted them.

"Forgetting about me already Tom?" I laughed boisterously. "Come on man, Beauty doesn't want to see that ugly mug of yours any more than I do" I joked.

I swung my arm around his neck and he buckled under the weight of it before laughing it off. "Jealously not a good look on you Beast!" he laughed as he tried to pry his head from my hold.

"Beauty's smarter than to be seen out in public with you man"

"Well that's fixable. We can stay inside" he winked and Seychelles burst out laughing.

"Get out of here you two" she laughed, "Beast, I'll be seeing you around" She winked and with a parting smile she turned to talk to a woman on another machine.

I watched her hips swing from side to side and realised Tom was ogling her just the same as I was. "Mm-mm-mm... she looks tasty" he murmured as we stepped out of the gym into the parking lot.

"Stay away from Beauty, Tom. I don't usually interfere on your conquests... but you keep away from her" I turned my eyes from the beautiful blonde bombshell back inside and stared down at Tom. The flustered and joking Ray from earlier was gone and back was Officer Beast. This Ray hadn't surfaced for a while and I flexed the muscles in my shoulders. "And that's an order"

His eyebrows lifted in surprise and he looked at me with calculating eyes but lifting his hands in defence. "Okay, okay... the girl means something to you. I get it... good choice Beast. To be honest, with a body like hers I'd be surprised if you hadn't had a roll between the sheets with her already. Or anywhere you could have her really."

Anger I hadn't felt in a long time coursed through my veins and I saw red. In a flash my fist shot out and caught Tom across the jaw. He dropped to the gravel like a sack of potatoes with an 'oompf' and immediately began groaning as he cupped his jaw in pain.

"What the f*ck Beast?!" he groaned.

"Don't you ever talk about Seychelles like that Tom. You're like a brother to me, but speak like that about her and next time you'll be unconscious!" I growled, furious at him even thinking that she would just be an easy lay.

"Got it man, geez. Don't get your panties in a twist" he rubbed at his jaw again and held a hand out, "Now help me up you pain in the a$s, I feel like more of your mom's cookies"

I rolled my eyes and grabbed his hand, hauling him up in one easy pull. He clapped me on the back and smirked at me before we hopped into my car and I threw him a wry look. "...what?" I asked dryly.

"You like the girl!" he sang, stringing out the 'you'.

"What? No, I don't" I kept my eyes straight on the road.

"Yes! You do!" he elbowed me lightly, "Aww, well ain't that sweet. Beauty and the Beast! Looks like I'm gonna be a god daddy sooner than I thought!"

"Shut up" I mumbled. "I do not like her like that... she's-she's just a friend I helped out"

Tom didn't reply and instead leaned back humming the tune that sounded oddly like 'Tale As Old As Time' with a smirk on his face.

Idiot.

I ignored him and instead concentrated on the road. The sun was shining brightly and the wind seemed ferocious today. Palm trees bent and their long branches waved in the wind. I continued to drive and soon the familiar peach house came into view.

I stopped the engine and we both stepped out. My mom was sitting on the porch and she looked up at the sound of the crunching of our footsteps on the shell drive way and smiled. Her smile soon dropped off her face when she looked at Tom.

"Tom! What in the world happened to you?" she asked with wide eyes.

"Oh you wouldn't believe what happened, Sandy!" he answered dramatically as he rubbed carefully at his already bruising jaw. "There I was... walking down the path when an out of control motorcycle came zooming down the road. A child was crossing the road at the time and without even a second thought for my own safety I rushed forward and threw my body out to push the child out of the way and the motorcycle clipped my face. What's a small bruise to the life of an innocent child?!"

"Well aren't you just the hero then Tom" my mom smiled at him chuckling lighly, "I know just how to celebrate! Come inside, I just baked some cookies!"

She turned and walked inside and Tom followed. Before he stepped inside he turned to me and raised his arms in victory, "Cookies!" he whisper shouted.

I rolled my eyes.

Idiot.

Seychelles POV

"Who in the world was that hunk of pure delicious muscles?" the woman I was helping out asked me after Tom and Ray left.

"My friend Ray was the giant and his best friend Tom" I chuckled lightly. I'd been asked the very same question about four times already while they were still here.

She purred appreciatively, "Is he single? I wouldn't mind giving him a roll between the sheets. I mean, if he's that big surely he's big everywhere"

I blushed and felt more than saw my face turn a horrifying shade of crimson. "Uh... I'm not sure"

She giggled and I smiled tightly before heading over to the showers then changed into a long, loose knitted sweater and leggings. I tied my hair up into a ponytail and slipped on a pair of flip flops before waving goodbye to the clients I passed.

I was exhausted. I had five personal training appointments today and I'd wanted to just head home but after walking into the gym earlier and seeing Ray there I couldn't help but stay. I felt goosebumps cover my skin at the memory of Ray when he carelessly shrugged out of his shirt.

He was magnificent. He was pure testosterone and a hard, muscled body that was only softened by the blinding smile framed by his to-die-for dimples. I remember feeling my stomach muscles clench and became all too self-conscious that I could have been drooling. The room became overwhelming hot and I had to go for a run on the treadmill just to calm myself down.

I parked my car outside my house and threw the door open only to be slapped by gusts of wind. I locked the car and entered my house making sure to lock that door too. The house creaked and howled louder than a pack of wolves. The wind forced itself into any cracks it could find and I knew I wouldn't be getting much sleep tonight. While it was windy back in town, it was even windier by the beach.

I heated up a ready-made meal in the microwave and collapsed on the well-used sofa as I reminisced this afternoon again. Tom was a funny guy. He was a dangerous flirt, but he seemed harmless enough. However, I couldn't listen to him and his corny jokes when Ray was just in the background flexing his many, many muscles.

The personal trainer in me stepped forward to readjust his hand placement on the bar and I seemed to be just hypnotized by him. I leaned closer than necessary because, weird as it sounds, the smell of sweat and something that could only be described as purely 'Ray' was intoxicating.

His hands were large and rough, full of work-hardened calluses that made me idly wonder how they would feel running over my skin. When I placed my hands over his to shift them slightly I felt a little flushed at being so close. I'd never felt so physically magnetised to anyone and the only word I could think of to describe how I felt being in such close proximity to Ray was overwhelmed.

I remembered watching every single part of his anatomy flex and strain as he pushed the weights up and down and...-

"Jesus, snap out of it Shell" I scolded myself. "He's just a guy... who saved your life... and despite his shot leg swam out to get you in the water and carried you all the way back to his home..." I sighed. "Oh God, I'm losing it..."

I finished off what was left of my pathetic TV dinner and cleaned up. The walls shook violently and I stared at the ceiling for a moment. When it didn't come crashing down or rip off I continued walking to my room and collapsed onto my bed - the only thing I actually splurged on. In the corner of the room I spied Sandy's clothes neatly folded and laid on the table.

I mentally reminded myself to go by her house tomorrow morning and return her clothes, and I wasn't sure why I was suddenly feeling eager to go to sleep and wake up to the new morning.

It wasn't because of Ray, it was probably because I was missing Sandy's addictive personality.

Yeah... my subconscious answered dryly in the back of my mind. You keep telling yourself that.

Chapter 7

Seychelles' POV

S I woke up later than usual to the howling and whistling of the torrential winds outside. The wind hadn't let up during the night and the house was freezing. I'd been woken up several times throughout the night and I was beyond exhausted this morning. The sun shone brilliantly and the scattered clouds flew quickly across the powder blue sky.

"Ughh" I groaned throwing my arm across my tired face. I tossed my sheets back and shivered as the cold clung to my exposed skin. I padded to the bathroom and grimaced at the woman who stared back. My hair was a muddle of tangles from endless tossing and turning and shadows dug deep around my eyes giving me a hollow skeletal look. Although still tanned from daily visits to the beach, my skin lacked its normal glow and instead looked pale.

"You look horrible" I murmured to my reflection before taking care of business.

I sighed when I realised I had nothing to eat for breakfast and mentally set a reminder to go grocery shopping. My stomach grumbled and I knew I wasn't being the healthy personal trainer I ought to be. The number one rule to being healthy and looking good was to eat nutritious foods. I sighed, I really should listen to myself.

Ignoring my grumbling stomach I quickly changed into a black bikini and threw on a pair of bleached denim short shorts and a white tank top before carefully packing Sandy's clothes into my bag. I grabbed a clean towel on the way out before locking the door and walked down to my favourite place in the world – the beach.

Since I woke up later than usual it was a bit strange to see the odd person walking or jogging across the wet sand when I was so used to the beach being void of anyone. I dumped my towel and bag on the soft sand before stripping off my clothes and running into the cold, glittering ocean.

As soon as it was deep enough I dived under and ignored the goosebumps that were plastered over every inch of my skin. Now this was a way to way up! The coldness of the water woke me up instantly erasing any trace of tiredness and fatigue and I continued to kick my way under the water further out.

When I could no longer hold my breath I kicked up and burst through the glassy surface of the water sucking in much needed oxygen. The wind prickled at my face and I smiled as I bobbed with the waves. I looked back at the shore and realised I was much further out than I thought and silently congratulated myself for having a better lung capacity than I realised.

"Jesus! I thought you were knocked unconscious again!" A deep male voice sounded from directly behind me.

I gasped and quickly turned to come chest to chest with Ray. "Ray! Christ! You scared the crap out of me!"

Ray ran a hand through his growing hair and chuckled lightly. "Sorry about that Beauty. When I saw you dived under the water and then not come back up I thought it was the surfing incident all over again" he shrugged looking a little embarrassed.

I smiled at his concern yet felt embarrassed that he kept bringing that up and lightly splashed him. "I'm a big girl Beast" I emphasised on his nick name, "I've been swimming and surfing since before I could walk. There's no need to worry"

We fell silent and once again I found myself gazing over his naked torso and lingering over his many, many scars. He was so broad up close (not that it wasn't obvious from far away) and I had the strange need to run my hands over his shoulders just to feel how strong they were.

I always did have a thing for broad shoulders.

"So... you come to the beach every morning then? I don't see you swimming when I'm out surfing" I commented paddling back a little when the waves pushed me closer to him.

He eyes wouldn't meet mine when he answered, "Uh... yeah I come here every morning. I'm used to waking up early, but this is only the second time I've been swimming since coming back"

I frowned, "So you go for walks?"

"Sometimes" he answered vaguely.

I laughed and splashed him, my hand coming into contact with his chest. Ooh that's solid. "Don't be so elusive, I'm trying to make conversation in the middle of the water here"

He cracked a bright smile and my heart skipped a beat when his famous dimples made an appearance. "I usually... people watch"

"Sounds reasonable" I granted him, though decided to change the topic since he was so vague about just being at the beach every morning. "You a good swimmer?"

He smiled and winked, "I'd give myself a nine out of tcn"

I laughed and kicked farther away from him. "Come on then. See my house over there? First one to swim parallel to my house then over to... that crooked palm tree over there" I pointed to an amusingly tall and zigzagged palm tree in the distance, "and then back to my house before swimming to the shore... wins"

He threw me a wry smile, "Okay... so, your house, crooked palm tree, your house then shore?"

"Yep" I nodded with excitement as the challenge became clear. He nodded slowly following the distance with his eyes before splashing me and swimming towards my house. I coughed and laughed hysterically, "Hey! That's not fair!"

I dove under the bobbing waves and stayed under for as long as I could before resurfacing again and stroking the smooth water towards the spot parallel to my house. Ray was barely ahead of me and I paced myself and controlled my breathing.

Once he was parallel he ducked under and disappeared. I felt a rough hand tug on my ankle and I laughed knowing it was the gentle giant. I ducked and flipped turning around in the opposite direction to swim to the crooked palm tree and as I swam was once again distracted by Ray's powerful shoulders and arms stroking and moving above the surface of the water.

Geez, he is powerful.

I was hypnotized by the tattooed dragon his back bobbing above the salt water then returning back under with every one of his strokes and I wondered how long it would take if I traced my finger over every tattooed line of it.

In a matter of minutes we were both swimming back to my house and I decided to end this competition already. I sucked in a deep breath and dove under the water and rolled my body to continue swimming as I kicked. I dipped under Ray's huge body and had to give him props for swimming fast for such a large man.

I popped up in front of him and kicked extra hard splashing him with endless amount of water before turning and ducking back underwater and swimming as fast as I could to the shore. My hearing was muted as I swam back and I couldn't help the smile that was plastered to my face.

I hadn't had this much fun in years!

The sand of the bank was shallowing and I stood up to run up. Water poured down my body and I collapsed onto my back on the wet sand laughing and gasping for air. I laid out like a starfish and waited a close to twenty seconds before Ray's heavy flopping onto the sand next to me was heard.

"Holy-sh*t!" he panted. A smile curved onto my lips again and I giggled. Giggled! "You're fast!"

"You're not too bad yourself Lieutenant" I winked turning my head to the face him. He was lying down like me, on his back with his arms and legs spread out. Every gasping pant he took his chest would rise up and down and I scolded myself for liking the sound of him being breathless. What is wrong with me?! "That was fun"

"Definitely" he agreed. Our gasping was slowing down and soon I was shivering while the winds blew against my skin. "Cold?" I nodded and looked over to my towel lying dry and scrunched on top of my bag a few mctres away and moaned at having to move. "I got it" I heard him say.

He rolled up and jogged away coming back with my towel and handing it to me. "Thank you!" I gushed and wrapped the warm fluffy towel around my shoulders. I noticed Ray was only in a pair of gym shorts and he sat contently beside me. His skin was covered in goosebumps as well but he didn't show any indication that he was cold.

I threw the other side of my towel around him so it wrapped around us both and he looked over at me in surprise. "Don't even try to pretend you're not cold" I rolled my eyes with a smile on my lips.

He thanked me and we sat together under my towel just 'people watching' as he put it earlier. We'd point out different couples and people making up stories for them and ended up laughing at how ridiculous it was for a particular man to be wearing a clear rain coat with the hood clasped around his head in the now cloudless sky.

"So no work today?" Ray asked as he flicked sand at my feet.

"Nope, no appointments today as far as I'm concerned. So I'm free unless I head into the gym" in the corner of my eye I saw him rubbing at his thigh again and I felt guilt swirling inside of me. "I'm sorry, I shouldn't have challenged you to a swim when your leg needs to be getting better"

He snorted and stretched upwards resulting in little clicking sounds from his stiff joints, "Don't be. I needed to challenge myself. I need to get back into shape as soon as I can for my physical exam before I find out if I can go back to the Air Force."

"Do you miss it?"

He answered without missing a beat, "Of course I do. It's all that I know. Of course I missed my mom the whole time I was away but... but the Air Force is my dream life. Most people don't understand. But..." he shrugged. "It just always was"

I closed my eyes and savoured the wind in my face now, "I think it's wonderful. It's your dream to help and defend people. That's the best dream I could think of"

He smiled but stayed silent but the silence was disturbed by his rumbling stomach. "Would you like to have breakfast at my place Beauty?" he paused and blushed, "My mom's been raving on about you..."

I chuckled softly, "Actually I was going to drop by after my swim this morning anyway. I needed to give back your mom's clothes she let me borrow" I pointed my thumb at my bag behind us.

"Sounds like a plan then" Ray stood up and wrapped the towel that was around him over me and I revelled in the warmth that lingered. He was so warm. He held out a scarred hand and I popped my much smaller one inside.

With one swift pull he pulled me up and I gasped as I flew straight against his hard, oh so very hard, chest. I splayed my hands against his chest to stop my head from thumping against him and pushed away clearing my throat a little. "Oh jeez, sorry Beauty" Ray stepped back and scratched his head making his biceps bulge at the movement. "I really need to realise my strength"

Laughing, I smacked his arm "Well that was a rush! Come on Beast, let's go"

He leaned down and picked up my bag before we both headed down in the opposite direction of my house. We were walking down the soft sand when he suddenly turned towards the trees at the back and turned his head to look at me, "This is my little secret"

It was then I noticed a break in the trees and the narrow path that seemed to cut straight through to the other side. Huh, handy. We began to walk down and I realised this was how he managed to carry me unconscious back to his house. Thank God for that! It cut down my guilt a little more knowing he didn't have to walk all the way around.

Within a few minutes the trees began to cluster closer together and when we pushed through his mom's adorable peach house was just down the path. The smell of baking wafted through the air and I instantly felt fuzzy inside. Compared to my breaking down shack that usually lacked in food and whistled and howled when the wind was too strong, Ray's home was warm and inviting.

I loved it!

We walked inside and I noticed the front door was un-locked and the smell magnified ten-fold the further inside we walked. I could feel myself drooling, what was that amazing smell?! I could hear Sandy's sweet laughter ring through the hall as a deep voice murmured something, apparently, amusing.

As Ray and I walked into the kitchen Sandy looked up and squealed when she saw me. "Shell! How lovely to see you, this was such a wonderful surprise. Sit down, have you eaten? I've just baked some muffins and there's some freshly baked croissants from earlier this morning"

Oh yeah, I loved it here! I returned Sandy's infectious smile and my heart clenched at the motherly love that she exuded. Motherly love was something that had been absent in my life for a long time and I found myself becoming addicted to it.

Chapter 8

I bit into another warm white chocolate and strawberry muffin moaning when the white chocolate melted on my tongue and I could swear I died and ended up in muffin heaven. Sandy was an amazing baker, and I assume cook, and I eyed the plate of different flavoured muffins, but took my time with this one so I didn't look greedy.

"These are delicious Sandy" I complimented her after swallowing a bite of pure heaven.

"God I miss these" Ray mumbled with his mouth full and grabbing another muffin. Sandy tutted him and smacked the back of his hand with her wooden spoon.

"I taught you better than that Rayray" she threw him an amused stare, "Don't talk with your mouth full" Ray swallowed and grinned childishly. I couldn't help but admire the sharp contours of his face and wait in anticipation for his dimples to peek through his cheeks everytime he chewed or spoke. "I'm so happy you came by Shell! I wanted to see how you were"

My heart constricted at how kind this woman was and I smiled warmly at her. "I was going to come by today even if I didn't bump into Ray this morning. I needed to bring your clothes back" I leaned down to snatch up my bag and eased Sandy's clean clothes out before showing her.

"Oh thank you! I completely forgot about these" Sandy walked around and I handed her the clothes. She excused herself and soon it was just Ray, Tom and myself sitting around the kitchen bench.

I wasn't sure if it was just me, but the silence was a little deafening and the short distance between Ray's arm and mine seemed to be electrified. What the hell was this feeling? It was so odd. I eyed the muffins again but decided to pass and instead spread some butter and jam on a croissant before biting into the soft bread.

Despite the booming business with the gym, I hadn't been able to spare much money for small luxuries like croissants and delicious tasting muffins. The money made from the gym went towards salaries and keeping everything spick and speck. The majority of the equipment was only a few months old and anything that wasn't was on the way to being replaced. I barely had money to do a big grocery shop let alone hire someone to fix up the house.

I would've been more than happy to play Miss Fix-It but I knew jack all about fixing a leaky roof and sealing cracks. I noticed Ray rub at his leg again and I felt guilt bubbling inside again. "Is your leg okay Ray?"

He turned his light brown eyes, the colour of autumn leaves, to me and smiled. "Yeah, a bit stiff and sore but nothing I can't live through"

Across the counter Tom snorted, "Bro, this is you living through it. You look like an old man when you walk. Get something done about it or suck it up man, I want you back at the base as soon as you can! The newbies were driving me nuts man!" Ray just rolled his eyes.

"I know a bit of remedial massage. I could help you out with it? It could help with the scar tissue as well" I nodded down at his muscled thigh.

"Damn! If I knew you were offering massages I'd have injured my groin" Tom joked while winking.

I saw Ray stiffen and threw Tom a menacing look. Tom smirked and shrugged his shoulders before going back to stuff another muffin into his mouth. Ray turned to me and offered me an apologetic smile. "Uh... It's okay Beauty. You don't have to, besides I'd normally have to pay for something like that"

I rolled my eyes. "Look, I'm feeling guilty okay? The swimming today, you having to carry me when I was unconscious... let's just call this me paying you back"

He was already shaking his head. "That's not something to have to be paid back for. I'm more than happy to have fun in a little competition and saving you doesn't require payment" he looked completely serious as he spoke the last part. "Besides, saving people is instilled in me"

"And helping people is instilled in me" I met his eyes. The way his autumn eyes held mine made the muscles below my stomach clench, in a good way, and after a few seconds he rolled his eyes and gave in.

"Okay, okay thank you. But I'll pay you–"

"No! Ray please, I don't want your money. I'm doing this as your friend" Friend... Before I could say anything more his giant, warm hand covered my mouth effectively cutting me off and he spoke again.

"If you won't accept my money, then accept my body" he finished. My face flushed and my eyes widened. What?! He paused, taking in my reaction. His face mirrored mine and the pulse in his wrist quickened before he withdrew it from my mouth.

"Woo Beast! What a way to get it on!" Tom guffawed in the background accompanied by his clapping.

"No... shit! What I meant was 'body' as in work-wise. I'll fix your leaky roof for you" Ray blushed as he glared daggers at Tom who only laughed harder.

"Is that what sex is code for nowadays? A leaky roof? Sounds kinda kinky Beast" Tom was practically crying in his hysterics.

I wasn't sure if my face was able to glow any more than the ripe tomato it was now... but apparently my blush could easily spread down to my chest while I stayed silent in my shocked and embarrassed state. His body? God, I thought he meant...

"Uh... sure" I squeaked, just wanting this whole discussion to be over with. "You can come around later to let me know what I need to buy for you to patch up the roof" I cleared my throat and looked around feigning interest in the wonderful paint work of the walls. This was beyond awkward...

"Oh, what'd I miss?" Sandy chimed as she walked around the corner. Tom was red faced from laughter and was wiping tears from the corner of his eyes while Ray and I just sat silently in our chairs and avoided eye contact for the moment.

"Oh... you had to be here Sandy!" Tom chuckled.

Ray's POV

"I will shoot you in your sleep" I threatened Tom slowly and angrily as soon as the door to the bathroom shut behind Seychelles.

"Hey, I wasn't the one who propositioned the lady" he held his hands up in mock surrender. "You're the one who was pimping off your body, not me"

I dragged a heavy hand over my face and breathed in deep before blowing out the breath. He's only here for a little while. He's only here for a little while. He's only here for a little while. I chanted in my head... but 'a little while' seemed like a long way away.

"I'm not joking, Shaw" I growled his surname, "I haven't shot a gun in a long while and right now my hand is twitching to leave a bullet hole in your ass"

Tom eyed me carefully and he sighed. "Alright, alright sorry. It must all the salty air here... and the fact that we're hours away from the base so you can't order me to run lapse or some shit"

I rolled my eyes and brooded on my stool as I crumbled the muffin between my fingers. Seychelles had gone to freshen up and my mom had gone to look for some oil so Seychelles could massage my leg. I wasn't so sure it was a good idea. Just the thought of her small hands rubbing themselves over my thigh was enough to make me stiffen slightly so I couldn't imagine how I'd fare with her physically doing it.

Ms Chenkins.

That's who I'll think off during the massage. Ms Chenkins was my least favourite teacher from high school. With body odour that seemed to waft around her and fill an entire classroom within seconds, I'm sure it was easily worse than being held hostage in a room filled with tear gas. She had the horrible habit of wearing faded floral tents and bending over way much in people's face...

I shivered. Yeah, that memory would work.

"Ready?" I turned around and my eyes zeroed onto Seychelles small figure leaning against the wall. She held up a bottle of rose oil, "Your mom said this was the only oil she had. She's also said she needed to go to the shops to buy more ingredients"

"I'll help her with that. Beast here ain't the only one who's strong" Tom jumped off the stool and winked. He grabbed another two muffins and strolled off towards the entrance. Once he stood behind Seychelles his eyes slid over her figure and gave me the thumbs up, nodding his approval.

"Don't you have somewhere to be, Shaw?!" I growled, hating that his eyes were able to slide over her curves.

"I'm going! Sandy! I'll be your personal helper for today!" He held his elbow out for my mom and she waved to the both of us before cheerily taking Tom's arm and closing the door behind them.

"So uh... where did you want me?" I asked, keeping my eyes on hers.

"Uh... Is the sofa big enough for you to lie down on?" her voice sounded raspy and husky. It was suddenly different before and even though it was subtle, it was easy for me to pick up. I had no idea what it was about this woman but I seemed to pick up on every little thing about her. She was just too easy for my eyes to wander over.

"To lie down on? No probably not, at least not unless my leg bends over the arm rest"

"Oh okay, so... your bed then" she stuttered over the word 'bed'. I nodded and led her down the hallway to my bedroom.

I pushed the door open and was suddenly self conscious about the old photos and books that lined across the shelves. The little airplane models that hung from the ceiling on thin wires that were presents from my mom every Christmas and birthday. My childhood bedroom was only salvaged by the weights and large yet old box television and the large bed. It was like a mix of the past and present together and I wondered what she'd make of it.

We walked in and when I turned around her eyes were gazing around the room and would pause over each photo frame before moving onto the next. "Your bedroom is very you. I like it" she smiled. "So uh... it'd probably be easiest if you were in a towel"

I nodded stiffly, of course, why hadn't I thought of that? I moved into the closet and picked out a clean white towel. I wrapped it around my waist and pulled my shorts down, letting it fall to the ground with a dull thud. I half wondered if I should keep my t-shirt on as well, but thought I might as well keep it on. Besides, it was my leg that was getting massaged not the rest of me.

When I strolled back into the room Seychelles had laid out some towels across my bed and singled out a pillow for my head to rest on. "Alright, so just lie down on your back here" she instructed me.

I did as she said and she came by my side rubbing oil over her hands. I watched the oil being slicked over her hands and through her fingers and quickly had to turn my eyes away. It's just a massage, for Christ sake!

"Okay, let me just reposition you a little bit" She pulled the towel up until my entire right leg was bared and one warm hand clasped my upper thigh while the other held my ankle. She tilted my leg a little so that my heel pointed to my opposite ankle and my knee bent outwards. "Oh-kay!"

A few drops of rose oil dotted my skin and I noticed her hands hesitate before she began to caress my skin and spread the oil. As she rubbed my thigh, the oil warmed up and soon she began to press harder. My leg would twitch as she circled her hands around the bullet scar from the front of my thigh but it was when she slowly began to make her way around to the back of my thigh that I felt my body heat up.

Her hands were like magic.

Slick with oil, her hands caressed my skin and massaged my muscles until I felt so relaxed I swear I was this close melting into my bed. I kept my eyes closed, feeling that if I kept them opened I would have nowhere else to look but at her sparkling emerald eyes. That seemed too intimate while her hands were stroking and caressing a place that was so close yet so far from where I needed it.

She began to concentrate on the scar at the back of my thigh and I felt my body grow hot. Good God she's so close, so close to where I desperately wanted her hands to be and...

Oh shit.

I felt the familiar stirring down below and my muscles clenching as I began to harden. Ms Chenkins. Ms Chenkins. Ms Chenkins!

Seychelles hands, so warm and hot was so slick and pressing in fluid circles up and around the back of my thigh.

Ms Chenkins!

I peeked through my eyelashes and instantly knew it was a terrible idea. Seychelles eyes were so zoned onto my upper thigh, a deep crimson flush painted her cheeks and down her slender neck while she used her whole body to push down with her hands to the bullet scar.

Ms Chenkins!

A wisp of blonde hair fell and kissed her cleavage. It stroked her flushed skin and at that moment her hands stroked upwards towards my growing er*ction.

Sweet baby Jesus, it's not working... MS CHENKINS!!!

I practically jumped out of my bed, clutching the towel in a bunch over my erection. "That was great Beauty! You have... magical hands... I feel great!" I was breathing hard and the room was electrified. Her eyes were dilated and her skin was flushed with a slight sheen of sweat shining across her chest. Through her bikini and white tank top her n!pples were hard and straining against the material.

I could barely drag my eyes away from the tantalising view. "Are you sure? I could-"

"No, no you were great!" I didn't realise I'd walked towards her until we were standing toe to toe and staring straight into each other's eyes. "Your touch is amazing" I whispered gruffly.

Our eyes bore into the other as the air seemed to thicken within our personal space. "Ray" she whispered.

"I should take you home" The words burnt my throat as they came out and I wanted to swallow them as soon as I said it. "Uh... Have a look at your roof..."

Seychelles blinked and stepped back clearing her throat a little. "Right of course" she forced out a little laugh. "You know... there's the annual beach bonfire tonight. I'm sure your mom would be there. There's a massive bonfire and families, teenagers, couples and singles all like to go"

She was rambling. I could tell it was a nervous habit and kicked myself for being the one to make her feel that way. "Will you be there?" she nodded. "Then how about I meet you there?"

I bent close to her, just needing to be closer. She smelt of sun and the sea. "Sure" she squeaked.

"Alright. It's a date".

Chapter 9

The drive back to my house was intense.

An intense silence and an intense electric feel buzzing in between us. I'd never had a previous experience like this before where all we had to do was sit next to each other and have sexual tension so thick I could possibly gather it, bake it and after eating it, have it go straight down to my thighs.

Which of course, was not the only way this sexual tension could get to my thighs...

I choked a little on the drool that had gathered in my mouth from the image of Ray between my thighs. Holy hell! Where the hell did that come from?! My face prickled from the blush gathering behind my cheeks and I quickly opened the window to let the salty wind cool me down.

"You okay?" Ray asked half amused and half concerned.

"Yep" I forced out, nodding quickly while avoiding his eyes. Instead I focused outside of the sexual tension filled car and gazed out at the white clouds streaking in almost perfect parallel lines. The bright rays of sunlight would peak through them and strike down at the ocean below like golden swords while the trecs swayed in the light breeze.

The texture of the road changed and grew bumpier letting me know that my shack of a house was drawing closer. Within minutes Ray parked the car and we both stepped out. Despite its run down appearance, I was glad to call it home and was excited to finally see it getting fixed.

"I'll just grab a ladder for you, wait here" I told Ray as I jogged over to the shed around the side. All my dad's old tools had been stored in the shed and it was easy to find the tall ladder leaning by the wall. I grabbed it and hauled it out.

As soon as Ray saw me he ran over, taking the ladder from my grasp, "Here, let me take that. The ladder is practically three times bigger than you" he joked. We walked side by side towards the house and I noticed that he didn't seem fazed at all by the heavy metal ladder. He strode tall and purposeful, he was confident with his body and it was almost as though the blushing, mama's boy was hidden away.

Ray set the ladder down and pulled it up, making it double its size, and leaned it against the edge of the roof. "I'll just go up top and check everything out. You go ahead and relax inside, Beauty" he winked and began to climb the rungs of the steel ladder.

My greedy eyes followed every move he took up the ladder and my ever ready blush resurface when my gaze dropped down to his tight behind. His jean clad ass was a sight to behold and I now understood the reason men loved to stare at the ass of any passing female. The saying 'he has an ass that could crack walnuts' really did come into reality as I stared up at Ray. Too soon he disappeared over the ledge, ending my ogling session, so I had no other choice but to head inside and get some paperwork done.

Fifteen minutes had passed and I was staring blankly at my healthy eating and daily exercise plans for a few of my clients when Ray came strolling in. He had a slight sheen of sweat over his forehead and down his neck before he brought the bottom of his t-shirt up to swipe it away. I was suddenly distracted by the washboard abs and defined 'V' that pointed straight down to his groin that I didn't realise he was talking to me.

"-don't need to buy anything"

"Uh, sorry what was that?" I coughed bringing my eyes back up to his.

"I said there are a few holes and other things that I can easily patch up on your roof. I'm pretty sure I've got all the materials needed back at home so you don't need to buy anything" Ray repeated himself with a smile.

"Oh! Great, well… if you're sure then I'd really appreciate it but if there's anything else just let me know and I'll buy it"

He nodded and scratched the back of his head, "If you want I can head home and come back here with the materials to get some of the work done. I'm not doing anything and I really could use with some physical work. I'm not used to all this lounging around at home"

This took me by surprise and I smiled eagerly. "Sure, I'm not going to complain!"

He winked and turned around heading back to the car, the car sinking down lower as he sunk into the driver's seat. "I'll be back before you know it!" he called out before driving away.

"Mmm" I purred watching the car drive away, "I can't wait"

This was torture.

Hours had passed and Ray had been up on the roof scraping and hammering away. I had basically locked myself indoors after checking up on him two hours ago and realised he'd taken off his shirt. The memory seemed to be teasing me, mocking me!

The sun had been beating down on his black and grey tattooed back, emphasising how broad and strong it was as he hammered down another nail. I never thought I would see a sight that could top it... until he turned around. I couldn't help the sigh that escaped my lips when his wide shoulders came into view. Each and every muscle was taut and strained as he worked and droplets of sweats lazily travelled down his body.

It wasn't fair!

I wasn't used to this kind of overwhelming sexual tension. I'd barely known Ray for long and here I was completely distracted by him. I threw the pencil down on the grid paper, knowing I was useless to try to make any sort of healthy plan and instead listened to the heavy banging coming from above.

Maybe I could sneak another look? Would that be creepy?

I decided to bring Ray a bottle of cold water and set about grabbing it before heading outside. He wasn't by the ledge and I couldn't see him so I decided to climb up the ladder to check how everything was going.

I was careful to climb up while holding the bottle of water and once I was over the ledge I couldn't help but stay quiet for a while. Ray was definitely made for physical work, his body was all hard lines and taut muscles. Wow. Just... wow.

I cleared my throat, "Thirsty Ray?"

Ray straightened and turned to smile at me, knocking the breath from my lungs, and wiped the sweat from his face. "Hell yeah. Thanks Beauty, it's scorching hot up here" he walked over and I handed the water to him before I watched his firm lips circle around the head of the bottle and gulped mouthful after mouthful of water.

I don't know how he managed to make even that look sexy! "You know... you've been up here for a long time. You didn't even really need to start working on the roof today. Why don't you call it a day and rest?"

He chuckled and sat down on the roof before pulling his t-shirt from his back pocket and laying it out next to him. He patted it waiting for me sit down next to him and I couldn't help but feel shy again. "I don't bite" he smirked. His eyes held mine and I could almost hear him in y head saying "... not if you don't want me to, anyway"

Sitting down on Ray's t-shirt I could still feel the heat from the roof seeping through the material and warming my backside. "You have a great view from here. I'm kind of jealous actually" he murmured quietly staring over towards the lapping waves of the beach.

"I've never actually seen the beach from this angle" I smiled enjoying the cool salty breeze as we both stared over the flat line of the horizon just soaking up each other's company.

It was really quite peaceful up on my roof, who would have thought?

A piece of paper blew out from his jean pocket and I quickly grabbed it unintentionally reading what was on it. It looked like a receipt and on it was a list of hardware printed. "Ray… what is this?" I asked curiously and confused.

His eyes fell onto the receipt and a blush caressed his cheekbones. "Uh… it's nothing" he replied as he tried to grab it. I moved away and continued reading the list before my eyes widened and I stared incredulously at him.

"Ray! These are all the materials you brought here to fix my roof! You weren't supposed to buy anything! You said you had them at your place and I said I'd buy whatever else you needed" Ray was so undeniably sweet! He had gone out and bought every scrap of material needed to fix my roof and he was planning on hiding it from me… not even looking for a thank you.

"It's okay… seriously. I owe you one for the massage. Just accept it because if you try to pay me back I will come back here and force you to take it back" he looked serious and yet there was a secret smile hiding behind his stare.

I bit my lip and smiled. "Well, that's very sweet of you Ray. I just don't want to feel like some charity case. I've worked so hard to get where I am now and I don't anyone thinking I need sympathy or want to get an easy way out-"

Ray's rough index pressed against my lips to stop me to talking, "You're not a charity case Seychelles. I did it because I wanted to. Just accept it, or you'll bruise my ego"

I couldn't help myself, my lips opened a fraction and my tongue flicked over my bottom lip and managed to caress his finger as I did. His eyes darkened and flicked down to my lips, watching my tongue slowly glide over them and his head moved slowly down as his finger slipped down to my chin tilting my head up. My heart skipped a beat, then another and then stopped completely as our eyes bore into the others.

A seagull squawked loudly behind us and with one blink of the eye themoment was over.

He blinked and removed his hand from me before clearing his throat and staring back out at the ocean, just as though that moment hadn't happened. Did it get hotter up here? Was the sun about to explode or was that just my face.

I glanced down at my watch just to have my eyes anywhere else besides the confusing and gorgeous man sitting next to me. It was four o'clock. "So uh, the annual bonfire starts at seven thirty tonight just little further down the beach. You still keen to come?"

I saw a slight smirk on the corners of his lips before it disappeared and a genuine smile appeared. "Of course. Can't ditch my date" he winked before his face straightened a little, "That is if you don't mind going as my date. We can go as friends if you like?"

"Hmm... would I mind going as the date of the man who saved my life and carried me through the heavy rain all the way back to his house despite his shot leg?" I asked sarcastically while pretending to think long and hard. I sighed dramatically, "I guess so!"

"You guess so huh?" he was crawling closer with a preda-tory smile on his lips and I had a bad feeling about that look. "Well how about I make it so that you're sure and not guessing"

Before I had time to think about what he was doing he lunged forward and began to tickle the crap out of me! My screams were tangled with laughter and he used his weight to pin my lower body down while he used his hands to tickle and touch me everywhere I was ticklish.

"Ray! Ray! No! I-I'm sure! I'm sure!!!" I laughed trying to kick him off.

All of a sudden the air was rushing past us and the choked curses from Ray managed to reach my ears while my belly did little back flips. Ray wrapped one arm around my waist and the other grasped the back of my head as he hugged me close and switched our positions. I had no idea what was happening until the hard thud of Ray's body underneath mine smashed our bodies together.

"Oomph!" we both choked out as the air was crushed out of us.

"What the-?!" I gasped

"Sorry! Completely my fault!" Ray apologised through his panting. I finally realised that while Ray was tickling me we had slipped down and actually fell off the roof!

"Oh my God! Ray! I'm so sorry!" I shrieked, "You keep getting hurt around me! I swear I'm some sort bad omen for you. Are you okay?!" I scrambled off of him and, despite how small I was compared to him, I tried to help him up.

Ray grabbed my hand but I didn't feel any of his weight as he pulled himself up. He was soon standing on his feet and wincing a little while he shook out his limbs "I'm okay Beauty don't worry. I've had much worse before"

I couldn't help but feel horrible. Every time we'd been together something always happened so that he ended up hurt. To my surprise Ray started laughing and pulled me flush against his body. I could hear the frantic thudding of his strong heart against his chest and the scent of crisp apples met my nose.

"It's never boring around you Beauty, I'll give you that" I could practically hear he smile in his voice and I couldn't help return his embrace while my smile melted across my lips.

It was getting late already and the sun was beginning its descent behind the horizon. The colours of the sky had begun to change so that countless shades of pink, orange and purple stained the sky. The parallel lines of the clouds above intersected the sky and changed the entire look of the sunset as the last rays of sunlight poked and rebounded through them. It was beautiful, without a doubt and I'd never seen anything quite as amazing.

Of course, watching it with Ray seemed to only perfect the sight before us.

Ray's POV

I wiped the condensation that clung to the mirror of my bath room and stared at the man who stared back at me. His hair was long... well longer than it had been for the last ten years anyway, and it actually suited him. His eyes, the colour of autumn leaves, were bright and excited.

As my eyes travelled down from his face to his broad shoulders and chest I noticed the many scars that had long stories behind them. Every long, short, thin and wide scar that marred his body proved that he had had his fair share of hard work and seen his share of war.

As I continued to stare at my reflection there was a thud against the bathroom door. "Hey Beast! I'm taking your mom down to the beach already! She says she wants to beat the crowd and meet up with her friends. She also says there'll be plenty of 'young ladies' there for me to hang with" I heard Tom shout through the wood separating us. I could practically hear his smirk and imagined that the 'young ladies' would have no chance tonight with him on the prowl.

"Sure, just don't be bringing those 'young ladies' to 'hang with' here under my mom's roof!" I shouted back rolling my eyes. The sound of Tom's guffaws had my chuckling as well and I brushed my teeth before exiting and walking over to my bed room.

Different styles of shirts and pants stared at me and I suddenly realised I didn't know what I should be wearing. I never really had this problem before and I was stuck on what was appropriate for a beach date. A grumble slipped through my lips and I reached over for a plain white button down long sleeved shirt and white washed jeans that were old but comfortable to wear.

I rolled the sleeves up and leave a few buttons undone. I glanced over at the clock and saw it was already quarter past seven so I grabbed my phone and wallet before slipping on a pair of flip flops and locking up the house.

The walk through the hidden pathway was dark. With the moon, stars and torch from my phone being my guide through the bushes and trees. I could hear the chatter and laughter from the crowds at the beach even if I couldn't see them yet and the smell of food cooking and burning wood reached my nose.

As I stepped through the tighter cluster of trees I spotted the crowd a little further down closer to Sechelles's house and I leisurely walked down smiling and nodding to the odd person. As I neared the giant orange and yellow bonfire I could see a group of girls crowded in a circle around Tom who was no doubt filling them in on his 'adventures' in the Air Force.

The group of girls began to laugh and giggle with Tom in the lead before his eyes landed on me. He raised his bottle of beer in salute and I returned his smile with an amused shake of my head. It seemed as though the entire town was scattered around the beach and the atmosphere was festive and happy. I began to search for Seychelles among the many people but it was a bit difficult in the dark.

Out of nowhere I was approached by an attractive woman with olive skin and black hair held up in a ponytail. She smiled at me brilliantly before handing me a beer from the cooler down by her feet. "Here you go Stud" I nodded in thanks and noticed she wore what a lot of the other women were wearing, which was simply a bikini top with either a pair of shorts or skirt of some sort. "I've seen you around the town lately, are you new here?" she asked batting her eyelashes.

"I grew up here actually ma'am, I've just been away in the Air Force is all" I answered her politely while still scanning the crowd. She was still talking to me and I was barely listening to her but all noise and chatter faded away when I spotted Seychelles.

She was standing behind the bonfire and looked as though she was looking for me as well. She looked stunning. She wore her blonde hair down and wavy and had no trace of make up on her flawless face. Her black bikini top peaked out from underneath the white sundress that hugged her chest before flowing freely around her waist.

My mouth went dry and I mumbled an excuse to leave the woman talking to me before making my way over to Seychelles. The light from the flames flickered around her face changing the angles and shadows around. I stepped around the fire and smiled brightly at her just as her eyes landed on me.

"Beauty" I called her softly, "You definitely live up to your nick name"

Her blush was enhanced by the firelight but she didn't duck her head. Instead her eyes trailed lazily from my eyes down my torso to my feet and then back up again. "You don't look half bad yourself, Beast" she replied with a soft smile. I held my elbow out for her and her delicate hand clutched it firmly. "Hungry?"

I chuckled and stared deeply into her eyes that reflected the stars twinkling in the inky black sky. "I'm always hungry"

Seychelles and I spent hours together laughing and talking together. From time to time we'd be interrupted by someone who wanted to talk to Seychelles or introduce themselves to me but we both seemed determined to keep to each other.

"Well, I'm heading back home Rayray" Sandy yawned behind her hand. "You look beautiful Shell darling, much more classy and your dress matches Rayray's outfit too" she grinned.

I blushed. "Mom…"

"Oh shush Rayray. I'm just saying. Anyway, you two have fun!" I bent down to kiss her on the cheek and she smiled happily before hugging Seychelles and waving as she walked away with her friends.

"Your mom is amazing" Seychelles breathed wistfully. It made me wonder what happened to her mom but it seemed as though now wasn't the time.

Almost all the families had gone home and the people left were either teenagers or couples around our age. The teenagers had cranked up their music and settled around the bonfire. The music was actually quite good and it had a reggae feel to it.

"Wanna walk?" I asked hopefully. I didn't want to hang around the rowdy group of teenagers. She nodded and wound her arm through mine as we walked down the beach enjoying the soft sand and the soft lapping of waves that mixed with the music.

The moon reflected off the remaining clouds and the stars were mostly hidden now but it was still beautiful. We were a little way away from the bonfire but still close enough to hear the music and I suddenly spun her around holding her hand. She squealed at the unexpected gesture and laughed happily.

"You dance?" she asked.

I snorted, "Not well, but I want to dance with you. If you want?"

She stepped forward against me and turned around so her back was the one pressing against my front and she pulled my hands down to her hips while she swayed them from side to side. I was hypnotised at the slow movements and began to sway with her to the reggae music in the background.

We danced together, learning how the other moved and swayed under the moonlight and I quickly spun her around. My hands caressed the soft skin of her shoulders and glided down to her hands before bringing them up to circle around my neck.

I was circled with her arms and I rested my hands back on her hips continuing our swaying dance. Anyone from the outside would think we were completely lost to the world and I had to admit that I seemed to be that way. The music had faded away, same as the waves, sand and wind. All I was focused on was the beautiful woman who was staring back at me and playfully absentmindedly with the hair at the base of my neck.

"This was the best date I'd ever had Ray" she whispered, "Thank you"

A slow smile crept onto my lips and I bent down so our lips were barely a hairline apart. "It was the best for me too Seych-"

I was suddenly cut off when two teenage boys started shouting and began rolling around the sand close to us as their fists began pounding into each other. The girls were screaming for them to stop but couldn't do anything to interrupt the blur of clenched fists. Their friends noticed the fight and instead of stopping them, they joined in.

One particularly muscular boy was running at them and tackled them, making them lose their balance and knocking them towards Seychelles. I quickly pushed Seychelles to the side and was barely missed by the brawling boys.

Now I was pissed.

Chapter 10

R ay's POV

"Hey!" I growled angrily. Since living back with my mom I hadn't felt an ounce of anger, but now I was definitely feeling it and I could feel my inner 'Beast' starting to emerge. The teenage girls looked up and I saw their mouths drop in silence; however the boys continued to tumble around in the sand. The sounds of fists hitting bodies and shouts between them persisted and soon one boy was fighting dirty by throwing sand around to distract his opponent.

"Hey watch it!" I heard Seychelles shout out. I turned to look at her and she was spitting out grains of sand from her sweet mouth and I growled. This wasn't how I wanted the night to end and I was beyond pissed off now. In a few long, angry strides I grabbed the fronts of both the boys' shirts and tore them apart, lifting them in the air so their feet could no longer touch the ground.

"What the fu-!"

"Hey! Piss off-!"

Both boys were shouting at me but I was way past seeing red. I threw them both to the ground and I could feel my nostrils flare with anger as I slowly stepped towards them.

"You'll be smart to head back home" I warned them quietly as my eyes bore into theirs. I had always been told back at the base that while my shouting could scare the mane off a lion, my quiet, calm threats would have had a ghost digging back into his grave.

Both the boys stood up with anger etched onto their bruised and bleeding faces. "Who the hell are you!" They both shouted angrily, though I noticed they didn't step any closer.

"I think the question here, boys, is who the hell do you think you are?" My eyes blazed as I remembered them nearly smashing into Seychelles. Their fight and the anger between the two seemed to have been forgotten as they and their friends stood in front of me; apparently trying to intimidate me with their numbers. I scoffed on the inside. "If you're planning on ganging up on me, I suggest you move along before I make you move along"

"Ray... I don't think that's such a good idea" Seychelles whispered from behind me. Her small, soft hand touched my shoulder but I was too used to having young men thinking they were tough and knew everything just because they could throw a punch. I spent years breaking that nasty little habit of theirs and I had an itch to do that again, now, with these teenage boys.

"These little boys don't scare me Beauty" I laughed, antagonising them even more. "They might as well pick up their tutus and go prancing back to mommy before their curfew is up"

I couldn't help it. I felt the familiar drops of adrenaline warming up my blood and if these boys wanted to tumble, then they could go ahead and deal with a real man. Maybe then they would think twice about fighting while they lick their wounds clean. A chorus of profanities were shouted at me and without a second glance over their way I threw my hand out to my left catching the fist of a boy as he tried to punch me without warning. Little did he know I practically had eyes at the back of my head.

"Looks like you want to be taught how to fight like a real man" I murmured.

I tightened my grip over his fist and used it to block the oncoming punch of his friend. I didn't want to actually hit the teenage boys. I was smarter than that, but there was never anything wrong with teaching them a lesson. I heard a mix of agonised shouts from the two boys and soon both their groups of friends were running at me in a pathetic attempt to overrun me.

The high pitched screams of the girls shrieking for us to stop seemed to turn into background noise as I turned and ducked under kicks and punches being thrown my way. It was twelve against one and... well, it slowly becoming less against me. I revelled in the angry adrenaline that had been dormant for few months now and felt the slightest sheen of sweat dampen my forehead. I used my forearms and shins to block and hit back, without too much force, as each boy attempted to land a fist or knee down onto me and it was easy to see that they had no sort of training in fighting or self defence. It was pathetic.

The muscular boy that had originally tackled the two fighting boys kicked my shot leg from behind and I fell to my knees automatically hissing at the pain from the bullet wounds. The remaining boys who hadn't backed away laughed quietly and stalked forward. I couldn't help the grin that pulled at my lips from their over confidence and swung my good leg out and around, effectively taking out their feet from beneath them.

As they thudded to the ground I jumped up and grabbed the backs of their t-shirts and hoodies. I had two in one hand and another three in the other and I dragged back towards the bonfire while they continued to struggled out from my grasp. With a little effort I tossed them forward and the teenage girls ran over to them, gushing over the bruises the boys were sporting.

I was breathing a little harder and it only added to the anger that was being portrayed by my angry glare at the group of teenagers. "I'm going to say this once more… I suggest you all get back home before I actually show you how a real man fights"

The muscular boy spat down at my feet, "You call what you did fighting! I could take you old man!"

I stared at him and watched his gaze falter slightly, "No. That wasn't fighting… that's what I call warming up"

Most of the group had left and there were only the five boys and their girlfriends staring at me as I glowered back at them. Seconds ticked by and after the urging of their girlfriends, they finally turned around with their egos deflated. I shook my head a little as I watched one of the boys push aside his girlfriend's hand as she tried to look at his bruised eye. "Some boys need to be taught how treat women properly… as well as others"

"Wow..." The sound of Seychelles' voice shook me out of my thoughts and I saw her wide eyed and staring straight at me with her plump lips slightly opened. I blushed. I hadn't wanted her to see that side of me, especially before we could actually get to know each other. I watched her chest heave up and down in shallow breaths and I was sure she was frightened of me now.

Seychelles' POV

Oh my God.

I knew Ray was strong, but I had no idea how strong and I knew he had a bad-ass side, but I had no idea how bad-ass. I could still remember how fast and swiftly he moved dodging and ducking hits as the twelve boys attacked him as though it was second nature...

... and it was seriously hot.

I felt flushed at watching his body move and how his muscles clenched and tightened. I was so hot and bothered that I mentally thanked the wind for being so chilly. My breaths were shallow and my hands were itching to trail over all the muscles that had just teased me. I had no idea how I could be feeling like this after watching him fight, but I supposed it was more of watching Ray's body movements than watching the actual fighting.

I raked my eyes over him and only realised after a few seconds that he was staring warily at me. "Beauty? Are you okay? I won't touch you if you're frightened"

Frightened?

"I don't... uh, what?" I mumbled.

Ray slowly walked towards me, looking as though I was a deer and would run away any second. I had no idea why... What I wanted to do was the complete opposite of running away; I wanted to press myself so close to him that the only thing between us was our skin! I blushed at where my thoughts were going and dropped my eyes to the soft sand.

I had to look anywhere else besides Ray because I just didn't think I could trust myself. The entire beach had cleared out now and Ray and I were the only ones left. The cold wind blew against my flushed face and cooled the perspiration that had dampened across my forehead and between my breasts. I closed my eyes and took a deep breath. Calm down, Seychelles! I angrily had to chastised myself.

When I opened my eyes I gasped at how close Ray was to me. Oh he's so close... if I leaned forward just an inch my breasts would be pressed up against his hard chest and- "Beauty?" Ray leaned down and placed a crooked finger under my chin tilted my face upwards so I had no choice but to look at him.

Hs warm eyes were soft as they gently caressed my face and when they landed on my lips I was done for. I moaned and leaned forward crashing our lips together and I swear I'd just died and gone to heaven. His lips were firm and yet soft at the same time and his hot breaths fanned my face. I melted into him and I couldn't stop my hands from reaching up and splaying over his wide, hard shoulders.

Ray finally seemed to relax after my shock move and a deep, primitive growl vibrated up his throat as his big, rough hands crushed me to his body. Oh my! A soft gasp escaped my lips when my knees gave way and if Ray hadn't been holding me so tightly I would have melted into a puddle and seeped into the sand below us. He took that opportunity to slowly push his warm tongue passed my lips and gently caressed my own tongue.

Goosebumps erupted all over my body and it had nothing to do with the cold wind whipping across my bared skin. I timidly massaged his tongue with mine and by the deep moan he emitted I knew he was enjoying our kiss as much as I was. Ray seemed to be taking over all my senses and I couldn't think. I could barely move and all I could seem to concentrate on was the overwhelming taste, sight, smell, sound and feel of Ray.

In the back of my mind I knew I was forgetting something, I knew it was important and yet I pushed it aside while I continued to taste the deliciousness of Ray Hodges. My head began to feel heavy and I started to feel a little light headed and before I knew it our lips were torn apart as I lost consciousness.

Oh right, I remembered now... I forgot to breathe!

Ray's POV

I stared at the unconscious Seychelles in my arms and just... continued to stare at her. Holy crap! I was rock hard and breathing just as hard all because Seychelles surprised me by doing the thing I'd wanted to do since I first saw her surfing in the water. It was something new for me, having a woman instigate our first kiss.

However, I never in a million years thought she'd pass out on me...

I was confused and just didn't know how to feel about that. Part of me felt proud that I could make a woman pass out from a kiss, while the other part was still shocked. She passed out on me?! "Beauty? Seychelles?" I spoke softly to her, pushing her hair out from her hair. She didn't respond but I already had a feeling that she wouldn't. "Looks, like I'm carrying you back home again Sleeping Beauty"

I knew that in retrospect, this situation would be hilarious. At the moment, however, I was still completely shocked. Somewhat numb. I fixed her so that I was carrying her bridal style and I looked around in case she dropped any belongings. Just her small bag that held her keys from what I could tell.

The moon was hidden by clouds which hid any reflections of light on the lapping water. The ocean was dark and, if not for the dying bonfire, the beach would be pitch black too. I limped across and up the small mountain of sand before I finally could see Seychelle's house come into view. "Thank God" I murmured. I couldn't stop the grin that was glued to my lips and reached into the small bag.

I managed to balance myself while holding Seychelles and unlocking the door and tripped slightly when I walked in. Using my elbow, I switched on lights to see where I was going and found myself wondering down a hallway to look for her bedroom. Her bedroom was the last door down the hall and I walked in before gently lying her down onto her big bed. She wasn't wearing shoes and only wore her white sundress so I left her as she was.

I pulled the blanket up and over her petite and very sexy body. It was chilly inside and I could hear the faint howling of wind as it blew into the house. A frown marred my face. Maybe I could come around again one time and try to fix up and holes so it wouldn't grow quite as cold at night.

I gazed down at Seychelles' sleeping form. Her eyes fluttered lightly as she dreamed and her bottom lip stuck out slightly. Damn, she was an amazing kisser. I bent down and hovered over her sweet lips, wanting just one more taste, but knew it wouldn't be the gentlemanly thing to do. I sighed and settled for kissing her cheek.

"Goodnight, my Sleeping Beauty" I whispered. Seychelles didn't stir. I left her bag on the bedside table and quietly left her house, locking the door behind me.

Despite the fact that we'd shared one kiss, I seemed to be addicted to Seychelles' sweet taste and one thing for sure was that that kiss would not be our last.

Chapter 11

Seychelle's POV

His lips were gentle as they slowly pried mine apart. His warm lips shot heated bolts of electricity from my lips and down my body. It made my heart stutter and warmth pool in my lower stomach as my toes curled once our breaths mixed together. The moment his tongue pushed past the boundaries of our lips and licked mine my hand shot up to his shoulders for support. How long had I known Ray for? Not that long... and yet one stroke of his tongue and I lost the ability to stand on my own two legs.

He wound his arms around my waist and pulled me hard against him. Every muscle of our fronts were touching and my neck had begun to strain from looking up. Suddenly he scooped me up and crashed us against the wall while my legs took a mind of their own and wound around his trim hips. A knot of tension was growing low in my stomach and my whole body jerked as he ground his hardness against me.

My eyes suddenly flew open.

What happened? I sat up quickly making the bed sheet fall from my shoulders and quickly scanned my surroundings. How did I get home? Where was Ray? It suddenly dawned on me that I was dreaming of kissing Ray... it wasn't real. I groaned in frustration and fell back into my soft bed. It felt so real! I was so sure I kissed him last night!

"Ergh... My mind is playing tricks on me" I mumbled to myself. I shivered slightly when the wind from outside blew around the house and stretched like a cat hearing my back crack. I noticed I was still wearing my sundress and as I stood up from my bed I tugged the straps over my shoulders and let it fall to the ground. I felt a little cramped and restless after my dream so I donned a plain black bikini and a surfboard before heading back down to the beach.

As I walked down the sandy dunes my eyes scanned the remnants of last night's bonfire. I couldn't help the smile that pulled at my lips as I remembered the events. Laughing and hanging out with Ray felt so easy, almost as though we'd known each other for years instead of a few weeks. The pile of burnt black wood sat on the sand and I knew later on it would be cleaned up. No one liked a dirty looking beach.

The sun was peeking out of the cracks from the cloudy sky giving off a purplish-grey hue to the clouds and I didn't hesitate to run into the cold water and splash through the waves before throwing my board down and paddling out deeper. This was what I lived for, the open ocean and nothing but freedom. Obviously the reality of hard work, bills and a broken house came rushing back as soon as I stepped back onto the shore but out here... out here I could let go of all my problems and concentrate on nothing but the lapping of waves and the wind kissing my face.

There was a lack of waves this morning so I settled for lying on my back on the board as I stared at the seagulls squawking above me just letting the water rock me gently. "It's quite nice out here when I'm not rescuing unconscious beauties" a deep, familiar voice spoke from beside me.

I smiled and then blushed as the memories of last night's dream came rushing back. "Good morning Beast" I smiled not looking at him.

"A very good morning Beauty" he chuckled. Finally looking over to him my breath hitched when I realised his face was just beside my board and his eyes were watching me intensely. Oh how I wish last night's kiss was real! He swam a little closer and placed his forearms on my board, resting his chin on top, "Last night was fun"

I blushed, "Yeah definitely. I think I fell asleep at the beach or something... I woke up this morning with no idea how I ended up in my bed" I frowned, "Did you bring me home Ray?"

"Yeah, I did" he suddenly looked uncomfortable, "You don't regret last night do you?"

I thought about it for a second. Last night... oh! The fight! "Regret last night? I'm pretty sure those kids deserved getting a little beating considering their attitude" I shrugged my shoulders, "Plus it was kind of hot seeing the angry side of yours"

He chuckled but looked confused, "Yeah I guess. But I was actually referring to after that"

I was getting so confused. I flipped over onto my stomach feeling the goosebumps spread over my skin as the wind hit the new wet part of my skin, "To be honest, I'm a little confused as to what happened last night. I had some pretty vivid dreams last night and don't know quite how to separate what was real and what wasn't"

Ray laughed louder this time. "Want me to remind you?" he had a cheeky expression and his eyes sparkled with mischief.

"Uh... okay?"

Suddenly he tipped my board over flipping me into the water with a cut off shriek. I spluttered as I broke the surface of the water and laughed uncontrollably hitting him with my fist playfully. He grabbed my wrist pulling me closer to him and held me between his body and my surfboard as his lips came crashing down. Oh my God! All the oxygen in my lungs came rushing out as my legs tangled with his. His lips controlled the kiss, pushing a little deeper with his tongue.

Oh wow. Oh wow, wow, wow!

Just as quick as he was to kiss me, he was pulling away and I found myself leaning forward to stay connected that little bit longer. My vision was a little blurry and I took a second to clear my throat and gather my wits. "Ah" I croaked. I cleared my throat again, "No... no I do not regret that"

He leaned down to peck me softly once more and let go of the board pushing himself a little further away. "Good... I don't either"

My body was so hot. It was burning from the inside and the cold water around me did nothing to ease the heat spreading from inside me. "Can I as you a question?"

"Sure"

"Did we only kiss the one time last time?" I knew it sounded a little odd, but I really needed to distinguish the difference between reality and my dream otherwise I'd make a complete fool of myself.

He gave a confused laugh, "Yeah just the once...? Because someone fainted. I have to say though... I am pretty flattered by your reaction" As if to match the heat in my body my face lit up and now both my body and my face were hot and flushed. Though for two completely different things! "Why?"

"Oh... no reason" I quickly answered. I looked at the sun in the sky and knew I needed to get to the gym soon. I'd lazed about yesterday and I needed to get back to reality, money for groceries didn't come for free. "How's your leg?"

I saw him shrug and lean back letting his body partially float and giving me a teasing look at his hard torso everytime his body bobbed a little higher than the water. "Getting better. I really need to up my training though so I can get back into shape before my fitness test to get back to the Air Force"

Two things flew through my mind once he stopped talking. The first was 'back in shape'?! Ray was by far the most fit and ruggedly ripped man I'd ever seen in my life and to think that he considered himself unfit now was laughable. The second thought was that he still wanted to go back to the Air Force. Why shouldn't he? He had told me before that it was his life and a kiss or two or three from me shouldn't change his mind. Not that I wanted him too.

"You know, I am a personal trainer who owns a gym and has credentials for deep tissue massage" I threw him a dry look. "I can help you, you know" His lips pulled back and shot me a brilliant dimple flashing smile that had me manually telling myself to breathe.

"I might just take you up on that offer then Seychelles" We stared at each other, I guess just soaking in the other's looks and presence but as the silence stretched on I was the first to break eye contact and cleared my throat.

"Well, you know where I am Ray. I think I should in now, I forget to check how many sessions I have today and I'm sure there's more paper work to be done" Ray nodded and together we paddled and swam back to the shore. He walked out first and jogged over to my towel only to jog back and wrap it around my shoulders.

The small gesture surprised me and touched deeply for some reason. The little things he did to make me feel more comfortable felt so out of place simply because I was used to taking care of myself. I dried myself off and he did the same but instead of parting ways as I thought we would, he picked up my board and walked along with me back to my house.

"So, if you have any spare time today I might just take you up on that personal training offer and uh... deep tissue massage afterwards if that's okay?"

"Yeah, sure definitely!" I wasn't sure why I sounded so keen. "I'll have to just check my schedule today once I get to the gym"

"I'll head there in a bit then" He smiled. He leaned my board against the side of my house and stepped closer to me. "I don't know what it is about you Seychelles... but, you seem to be a magnet to me" He towered over me and I pressed my back against the wall, he smelled of apples and sea salt and while that seemed like an odd mix, it was heady and hypnotising.

I could see he wanted to lean down and kiss me again, hell I wanted him to! But he closed his eyes tight and clenched his fists before backing away and smiling politely to me. "I'll catch you later Beauty" With a wink he turned around and walked back down to the beach.

Damn, but that was a beautiful sight.

I sighed and turned to walk inside my empty house. After a shower and a quick breakfast I was out the door and started the engine to my car before driving down the driveway. As I drove through town I gazed at the smiling couples, both young and old, and wondered if there was a chance I could have that with Ray. I laughed and shook my head, there was no point.

"He's training to get back into the Air Force, you idiot" I murmured to myself, "He's freaking asking for your help to eventually leave this town. There's no point in even trying for a relationship with him" But there was no harm in dreaming about one.

Ray was every woman's dream. He was sweet, kind, loving, generous and honest. He loved his family and his country enough to risk his life in the Air Force and it didn't hurt that he was devastatingly handsome with a smile and body to die for. Sex on legs... very long and powerful legs. He blushed at compliments and yet could fight several people at once. In the short amount of time I'd known him I've seen different sides to him and I liked every single one.

I arrived at the gym and parked my car in its usual spot before walking inside. Naomi was spinning around on her chair and blowing a bubble with her gum. "Morning Mimi" I laughed.

"God Shell, I'm so bored!" she whined.

I couldn't help rolling my eyes, "Well then do something. I'm not paying you to be bored"

She stuck her tongue out at me but continued to spin around anyway. In reality, I didn't need a receptionist five days a week. The only reason why I hired her for that many days was because she desperately needed it. She was a few years younger than me but I knew that she'd gone through much more than what some other women do in their life. So when she refused to stop begging me for a job, despite my own financial issues, I hired her for five days a week and have never regretted it since. I walked to my office, greeting the regulars on my way there, and dumped my bag onto the ground before scanning my schedule.

I had a session in an hour and another two just after lunch. I mentally noted it down then grabbed Ray's file out to search for his number. I bit my lip and stared at his number before saving it into my own cell phone, I mean... we were friends after all. It wasn't creepy... I sat back as I listened to his dial tone and waited for him to pick up. He didn't answer, instead it went to voicemail and I felt a little disappointed when I left him a message instead of talking to him. I told him I was free after two o'clock and I couldn't help feeling excited at working with him again.

Today. Was. Going. So. Slow!!!

Throughout the day I found myself checking my watch over and over and when I thought that fifteen minutes had passed, it had only been one minute. Ray had called me back saying he'd meet me at the gym and when my last session before Ray's finally finished I felt like a giddy high school girl again. I didn't know what was wrong with me and I had no idea why I was acting this way but I knew deep inside it was because I hadn't had a relationship in years that a simple kiss was a big deal for me.

I was floating around the gym, just giving tips and helping members that wanted it when Tom's happy voice shouting from the entrance. "Shell! Long time, no see!" he grinned walking straight up to me and wrapping an arm around my shoulders.

I laughed with a shake of my head, "Hi Tom, as I recall I saw you last night with a hoard of young girls hanging onto your every movement"

"Now, now there's no need to be jealous Shell, there's enough Tom to go around for every beautiful woman. And by 'beautiful woman' I mean every woman" he winked at the woman I was helping.

"I highly doubt Seychelles is jealous of your many con-quests Shaw" Ray's deep, voice added. I looked over and saw him wearing an amused expression. "Hey Seychelles"

"Hey Ray..."

Tom looked between the two of us before he unwrapped his arm from my shoulders and pretended to choke as he coughed dramatically, "Damn! The sexual tension between the two of you is so thick I can barely breathe!" A deep blush instantly coloured my cheeks and Ray's face mirrored mine. Wow, the uncensored mouth of Tom Shaw was ridiculous. He never held back anything he was thinking!

"Uh, come on Ray. Let's get started yeah? Feel free to use the machines Tom" I called over my shoulder to Tom who had already taken my spot in helping the same woman he winked at out.

"I'm so sorry Beauty. Tom... he doesn't have a filter" Ray grumbled adorably.

"That's alright. Here, I'll get you to warm up on the tread-mill first, then I want to focus on your legs today since that's where your injury is and would need to be worked the most" He nodded and just like that we fell back into our comfort zone.

Ray's POV

Who knew the tiny blonde with a stellar smile could be such a killer!

I hadn't had a hard work out like today's session in months and my aching leg was proof that Seychelles was in her element. She'd started off easy enough but as the minutes ticked by she'd stepped into her personal trainer mode and pushed harder and harder until I was at my limit and kept me there. She'd told me that we'd work my legs, and they were worked!

"How are you feeling?" She grinned with a lopsided smile.

"Beat" I chuckled. "I'm not going to lie Beauty, my legs are killing me especially my shot leg. You definitely rode me hard"

As soon as I said the words I wanted to swallow them back down. I could just imagine her riding me hard, and right now was neither the right time nor the place to be having thoughts like that. She didn't seem to notice though as she laughed and threw my clean towel at me. "So, with your uh deep tissue massage, did you want me to come around to your house later?"

I could feel a stirring in my gym shorts at the thought of her hands on me again. Not only did it feel amazing last night she gave me a massage but I felt much closer to her. "Uh no, I'll swing by yours later. I could bring dinner and have that massage afterwards?" I asked with raised brows.

To be completely honest with myself, I wanted something with Seychelles. She was daring, hard working and had such a big heart that I couldn't help but want to explore this relationship with her. We clicked so well when we were together and our kisses... wow. I wanted more of those, but I was a kind of guy who wanted to be involved with a woman when I kissed her.

"Oh, you don't have to Ray. You can just come afterwards" She declined but I shook my head.

"Nope, no can do. I'll be over at your place at eight with food. See you then Beauty" I winked and strode past Tom dragging him away from another woman he was trying to impress. With a quick glance back at Seychelles before we left the gym I saw her biting back her smile. Hopefully she was as excited as I was to see her again.

"I could get used to this place" Tom sighed as we passed a group of girls in cropped shirts and short shorts. I ignored their giggles and coy looks and thought about what he just said. I could get used to staying here as well, especially since meeting Seychelles. But my life was the Air Force, I knew everything that about it and I was good at what I did.

I spent some time with my mom and Tom back home and once seven o'clock rolled around I left to buy dinner and drive over to Seychelles' house. I waited outside her door holding two pizzas and a grocery bag with soda and dessert. After today's session I needed food! Seychelles opened the door in a matter of seconds wearing a loose, white cotton t-shirt and grey cotton shorts. Her long blonde hair waved over her shoulders and her emerald eyes sparkled with happiness.

"Hey Ray, come on in" She smiled. She led the way inside and I couldn't keep my eyes from her ass. They were perfect round globes that swayed from side to side with every step and I almost ran into her when she suddenly stopped and turned around. "I love pizza!"

"I hope you're hungry because I am starved! You really know how to work a man and make him hungry" Once again I wished I could swallow my words. I wasn't sure if I was just saying phrases that had sexual innuendos or it was just me thinking that way. In any case I really needed to stop.

"What's this?" She asked pointing at the grocery bag.

"Soda and ice cream for dessert"

"I could just kiss you right now Ray!" She beamed clapping her hands together. She put the ice cream away in the freezer and I stepped up right behind her.

"Well, I'm not stopping you Beauty" I whispered in her ear making a wavy tendril dance. She turned around and our eyes clashed again. Could she feel that connection? To my surprise she stepped up on her toes and gently brushed her lips against mine so lightly I would've second guessed if she really did kiss me.

"Thank you" she whispered before ducking into the lounge. She placed the pizza and sodas on the coffee table and turned the volume up louder. "Come on Beast, or I'll eat everything!"

"Damn! Where do you put all that food?!" I cried in amused shock. Seychelles and I had both eaten a pizza each and I more than surprised that she could keep up with me. "I love a woman who can eat!"

"And I love a man who can bring me some ice cream" laughter bubbled up my throat and the look Seychelles was giving me was priceless. I stood up and grabbed the ice cream along with two spoons and fell back down on the sofa handing her one spoon.

We watched a movie on the TV while eating the ice cream and it just felt so... normal. It felt like I could do this every night. "You have a little something on your lip" I pointed at her with my spoon. She swiped around her mouth but kept on missing it so I leaned forward and held her hand to direct her where it was. Once she wiped it off I didn't even think twice before bring her hand to my mouth and sucking the ice cream off the pad of her thumb.

Her eyes dilated as she bit her lip and I noticed her chest rising and falling much quicker. It was only then did I realise what I doing. My hand traced around her wrist and up her smooth arm before I caressed her jaw line. "Seychelles... I'm going to kiss you again".

Chapter 12

R ay's POV

I couldn't hear anything but the heavy thud thud of my heart and even if she said anything, which she didn't, I wouldn't have heard her. Her lips were slightly spread apart and her pink tongue darted over her bottom lip to wet it again. I begged her with my eyes and with a slight nod of her head I pushed forward and grabbed the back of her head, feeling her silky strands gather between my fingers and I pulled her towards me.

Her breath was short and hot and I just wanted to breathe the same air as her. I don't know what it was about her but I wanted her. I wanted to know every inch of her smooth skin and every dip and hollow. I bit her bottom lip between my teeth and ran my tongue over it before sucking on the plump skin. I could hear her breathy moans and feel her small hands shaking on my knees. She widened her lips a little unconsciously inviting me into her mouth but I held back. No, I wanted to explore every bit and savour every moment.

I nibbled at her lip until the blood underneath swelled inside and kissed both corners, slightly tasting the ice cream she was eating earlier. I was playing with fire, my own hardness was pushing so hard against the material of my jeans I shifted slightly to ease how uncomfortable it felt. Seychelles was moaning in frustration and with a quirk of my lips I kissed her fully. I could never get used to how soft her lips were and how well they moulded with mine.

Our lips toyed with each other and after a minute of teasing her and her open invitation for more, I finally slipped my tongue through her lips and tasted her. Moans escaped from the both of us but and the more I tasted her, the more she pushed harder against me to taste more of me. The room began to feel hot but neither of us seemed to care. I tightened my hold in her hair and she tightened her grasp on my thigh making my already throbbing er*ction jump in need.

I pulled back and gasped for air, just as she did, and slowly moved back before collapsing at the back of the sofa. Damn, she was an amazing kisser! My groin throbbed painfully and I quickly covered it with a pillow. Seychelles' hair was all over the place, her face was flushed and her lips red and swollen while her eyes were glazed over. She looked utterly stunning and the only way she could look better was if she was on her back and stripped from her cotton barriers.

I would shoot myself in the leg again just to see her like that.

"Wow" she croaked, her eyes focusing again. "Feel free to do that whenever you want Beast"

"Oh... I have free permission now do I?" I smirked. I was glad she seemed to pull out of her daze and look so unfazed. I was still reeling a little bit. She nodded with a blush and stood up dusting off invisible dirt from her shirt. I couldn't help notice the hardened nubs poking through her material and felt ease that at least I wasn't the only one affected by our earth tilting kiss.

"So how about that massage Lieutenant?"

I glanced down at my lap and gulped, thinking of my high school teacher Ms Chenkins again to get this hard on down. "Uh... yeah in a minute"

She threw me a confused look but her eyes wondered down to the pillow covering my lap and her face lit up like the fourth of July. It was a beautiful colour on her skin.

"Oh okay, sure. I'll just uh... I'll be right back" she mumbled and turned to walk into the hallway.

As soon as she was out of sight I threw the pillow aside and stared at the tent in my pants. "I know! I know she's ridiculously good looking and has a mouth to die for but you need to disappear!" I whisper shouted at my crotch. "Now is not the time!"

I sighed and leaned back thinking of everything from high school algebra to training back at the base and eventually it worked. I stood up and wondered where Seychelles was hiding and walked down the hallway. I walked past her room only to walk back again and saw her sitting on her throwing a sheet over her bed.

"Need some help?" I asked making her jump.

"Oh! No, no I'm fine. I'll just grab the oil and while I do that you can get ready like last time. There's a towel here for you" She quickly walked out of the bedroom closing the door behind her and I quickly stripped off my jeans and wrapped the towel around my hips. A tentative knock sounded at the door and I shouted for her to come in.

She stood smiling in the doorway and walked in gesturing for me to lie down. I followed her instructions and watched her slather the oil over her hands, I just hoped I had enough will power to keep my er*ction at bay this time. She positioned my leg the same as before and this time, instead of staying quiet, she began to talk to me. We spoke about her house, my mother and Tom, we spoke about her gym and all the other safe topics that kept away from us.

"How's the rest of your body Ray?" She asked me softly.

"A little sore, I guess. Especially my back" I mumbled. Her hands were magical and I was beginning to grow sleepy.

"I can massage the rest your back and shoulders if you want?" she whispered.

"That'd be amazing, Seychelles. I'd owe you one" I slurred. Her hands traced my lower stomach just above the edge of the towel and goosebumps erupted all over my skin as she slowly pulled my shirt up. In the back of my hazy mind I laughed mentally at how this role seemed to be reversed. Usually I was the first one to remove the woman's shirt, not the other way around.

I lifted my body up for a moment to help her take off my shirt and she instructed me to turn around onto my stomach. I heard her slight intake of breath and nearly jumped out of my skin when her finger lightly trace over the swirls and lines of my tattoo. She squirted more oil onto her hands and began to rub them over my back, massaging and easing out all the knots. Before I knew it my eyes slid shut.

"Take cover!" I shouted as another round of bullets came flying through the air. Tom had been hit by a stray bullet, I wasn't sure whether it was enemy or accidental friendly fire but I'd risked my own neck running out in the open to drag his bleeding body to safety.

At an interval between shots I jumped up and began to fire at the enemy. A bullet grazed my ribs and I hissed in pain but otherwise ignored it. I'd managed to shoot down five men but they seemed to be getting in lucky shots when another bullet grazed my arm. An angry shout came from my left and I quickly dodged the man with a knife. I squeezed the trigger as I aimed the gun for a clear head shot but realised I was out of ammo.

The man lunged at me again and caught me off guard as the blade of his knife slashed across my chest. Using the butt of the gun to strike him down I kicked him away and ignored the streams of blood flowing down my body as I dragged Tom deeper into cover.

I snapped my head up with my heart thudding fast and loud in my chest and sighed in relief. It was just a dream – a memory, but a dream. One of the many times I'd ended up with a scar decorating my body. Seychelles hands stilled and laid on my back as she peeked over to me. "Are you okay Ray?"

My eyes darted to her and I don't know what it was, but I felt overwhelmingly relieved to see she was safe. It wasn't as though she was in my dream, or even in any sort of danger, but I turned and sat up before dragging her close into a hug. I breathed in her scent and felt myself relax. I never needed anyone to relax or felt like this over anyone besides my own mother and it was surprising.

Seychelles timidly hugged me back and stroked her fingers through my hair. "You okay?"

I nodded but pulled her down to lie next to me on her bed. I needed her, and I wasn't one hundred percent sure why. I crashed my lips down to hers and, unlike our kiss in the lounge, I didn't wait to plunge my tongue into her mouth to taste her. I pulled her close to me, crushing her tiny body against mine but she didn't complain. She pushed and pulled me closer as though she needed me as much as I needed her.

Our kissing deepened and intensified. There was an amazing chemistry that just seemed to sizzle between us like electricity and when we touched or kissed that electricity sparked like tiny fireworks bursting across our skin. I flipped her over and ground my raging hard on against her just needing to ease some of the discomfort. I broke our kiss and began nibbling and biting down her jaw line to her neck, tasting the soft skin.

Her soft mews of approval set my blood on fire and before I even realised what I was doing I pulled away from her and hauled myself off the bed breathing in ragged breaths. She sat up with her hair tumbling everywhere with her eyes dilated and the smell of our lust filling the room. Her eyes shot me a questioning look while she breathed heavily, almost as though her lungs were desperately trying to take in enough oxygen to talk.

"Ray?" She panted.

"I'm sorry Beauty... I shouldn't have done that. You deserved far better than that." I groaned rubbing my eyes with the heels of my hands. I was very aware that the towel was sporting a very desperate tent between my legs but I already knew that I wouldn't be able to do anything about that any time soon. "I... I think I should go, Seychelles"

I grabbed my jeans and discarded shirt pulling them on quickly before throwing the towel into the hamper in the bathroom. "Ray... it's okay. I wanted you to... I-"

"No Seychelles, I'm going about this all the wrong way. But don't worry... I'll get it right" I promised before grabbing my keys and driving away cursing myself and my damned too-eager body.

Seychelle's POV

What the hell just happened?

What. The. Hell. Just happened?

I stared at the empty doorway and felt my brain give up trying to rationalise what the hell just happened. I flopped back onto my bed and stared at the ceiling. One moment we were locked in a steamy make out session, all I could think of and feel was Ray. He seemed to be everywhere. He was intoxicating and felt like an addictive drug that I couldn't seem to get enough of.

His skin was soft, yet rough, and so very, very hot. I couldn't have helped splaying my hands over the muscles in his back if I tried. I touched my tender lips with my fingers and closed my eyes remembering our kisses; his slight stubble rasping against my skin and leaving my face and neck tingling with its memory. Ray definitely had a way with his lips and tongue and I bushed at the thought of them kissing elsewhere on my body.

If he hadn't freaked out and left.

A million thoughts were running through my mind and I couldn't seem to concentrate on just a single one. I wondered what made him panic when he woke up in the first place and what made him stop kissing me just before he left. He had left me feeling confused and utterly wound up.

'I'm going about this all the wrong way. But don't worry... I'll get it right'

What did he mean by that? He's going about it all the wrong way? He'll get it right? "Ergh!" I groaned and kicked at the sheets. "Ray Hodges, you are one mysterious and confusing man"

I walked into the gym feeling a little less energetic than normal. I didn't see Ray on the beach this morning which is probably the reason why I felt so sluggish and down trodden. I wondered if he thought I'd be angry at him or feel awkward, but I wouldn't feel that way at all. Even if he thought it was all a mistake and didn't want to be anything more than friends I would've still wanted to see him. He had a charismatic personality and I could see us being friends, as much as that word felt a little bitter on my tongue, in the future.

"Morning Mimi" I murmured before quickly walking into the office. I stopped in the doorway with wide eyes when I saw the bouquet of long stemmed blood red roses sitting on my desk. "What the...?" Curiosity got the better of me and I excitedly dashed over to it and opened the little card that sat in the middle.

Beauty,

Please forgive me for last night. Not only did I freak out on you but I left you suddenly without a proper goodbye.

I don't know how you feel about 'us' or if there even is an 'us', but I want to explore this chemistry we have... I know you feel it too Seychelles, please let me make it up to you.

Meet me tonight at nine o'clock on the beach where the bonfire was. There's something I want to show you...

Waiting,

Beast

I squealed, a Cheshire cat grin pulling at my lips so hard that my jaw began to hurt. I felt hope blossom in my chest at the realisation that he wasn't brushing me off and it was quickly replaced with excitement, anticipation and curiosity. I suddenly had a little too much energy, I couldn't sit still for the life of me and since I didn't have any appointments today I decided to leave and spend the day running errands to make time run faster.

Nine o'clock seemed so far away and the anticipation was killing me already!

Chapter 13

Oh man, what the hell am I supposed to wear?!

It was quarter to nine already. I was freshly showered and had been standing at the mouth of my wardrobe for the last fifteen minutes staring blankly at the different clothes hanging on their hangers. I moaned and groaned in my head, I hated being a woman sometimes! It was confusing to think up an outfit for a date when there were so many possibilities.

I sighed and shook my head. Ray had seen me during my worst and I was running out of time already. I walked in and searched through my clothes and was surprised when I saw a dress I hadn't seen in a while. It was a light green dress with a pink floral pattern covering it. The back of the dress hung low while the front was cut just below mid thigh and came with its own pink belt. I recalled buying it on impulse just because it was so adorable in the store but hadn't had actually had the chance to wear it.

I quickly pulled it on and grabbed my white shawl to fend off the wind from the beach and tied my hair up in a messy bun letting a few wavy tendrils fall about my face. I didn't bother with makeup, I never usually did, and decided to forego wearing shoes. With a quick glance at the clock I saw it was already nine and I was running late, so with one last glance in the mirror and no time to change I dashed outside locking the door behind me.

I kept an eye open for Ray but there was no need. He was on the beach just below my house and looked breath taking in beige pants rolled up and a white linen shirt that was left open showing me his impressive chest. His smile widened when he saw me and his dimples made an appearance. I could've melted right there. I carefully made my way down to him and once I was within reach he held a hand out for mine and kissed the back of my hand.

"Hey Beauty" he straightened up and spun me around catching me by surprise, "Beautiful just doesn't compare to how you look"

I blushed and bit my lip shoving him playfully with my shoulder, "Stop it, Ray, you'll make my ears bleed if you spoil me with compliments like that"

"They're facts Seychelles" Hesitated for a moment before leaning down and pecking me on the corner of my mouth. "Come on... I have a surprise for you"

He tucked my arm in the crook of his and together we walked barefoot across the soft sand. It was a clear night. Not even a cloud dared to mar the star filled sky tonight. One of the pros to living in a small beach town was that at night time there wasn't enough lights to disturb how wondrous the sky was. Most people never got to see how many stars there actually were and how they glittered like diamonds against the velvety sky. Tonight, because there were no clouds, and the waves were still nonexistent, the sky seemed even larger since it was reflected perfectly across the ocean.

The moon was a pale silver crescent and watched down on us silently as we walked in silence. It wasn't an awkward silence at all either, it was a comfortable hush that fell over two people who felt at ease around each other. I breathed in the chilly salted air as it kissed at my face and exposed skin and wondered where he was taking us.

The warmth from his large body stretched out and warmed my left side as we walked and I couldn't help but walk closer to him seeking more of his heat. He began to slow down and stopped, seemingly nowhere interesting. He let go of my arm, leaving me feeling cold once again, and walked over to the bushes pushing them aside to reveal the hidden path I forgot all about.

He nodded his head in the direction of the path and held his hand out to help me through the barrier of bushes. Once I was through he pulled out a scarf and walked behind me, "I'm going to blind fold you okay? It'll ruin the surprise if I don't" He told me, though it sounded more like a question. He was asking for my trust and I chuckled knowing he hadn't figured out that he had my trust from the beginning.

I nodded and stood still while he tied the scarf firmly but gently across my eyes. I was blinded and saw nothing but blackness. It heightened my senses and now I was even more aware of Ray's searing body heat that contrasted so much to the chilly wind that whipped around us. Goosebumps erupted everywhere and my n!pples puckered when I felt his lips kiss gently at the back of my neck and his hands firmly clasped my hips bones.

I wasn't sure if he was meaning to, but with his simple touches I felt an invisible tug from my n!pples to my the apex of my thighs and I let out an airy gasp. His lips moved slowly to my ear and he grazed my ear lobe between his teeth, "Ready?" he whispered, his warm breath sending another bout of goosebumps over my skin. I nodded. "Trust me?" I nodded again and moaned when he kissed the sensitive spot below my ear.

He could very well kill me with his barely-there kisses, I was sure the anticipation of 'more' would be the death of me!

He stayed behind me and gripped my tighter, making me jump and the warm pooling in my lower stomach stir once again, but began to push me as he steered me where to walk. My feet sunk into the cold soft sand, occasionally feeling a hidden shell, while the smell of Ray, apples and sea salt, floated around me making me feel heady.

"Are we nearly there?" I whispered curiously.

His thumbs circled just inside my hip bones, "Almost there, baby" I bit my lower lip at being called 'baby'. I'd never usually liked being called 'baby' but the way he purred it in my ear made me want to throw him down on the sand and run my tongue over every inch of his body. I was painfully aware that my n!pples were leading the way and hoped the floral print of my dress hid it enough.

Suddenly Ray stopped steering us and let go. "Keep the blindfold on okay? Don't take it off until I tell you"

My lips curved into a smile at his anxious yet excited tone and I nodded my head. His body heat vanished from beside me and I could hear the slight crunching of sand beneath his feet as he walked away. I was so curious what he could be showing me in the middle of the bushes but he sounded so excited I held back my hand from tearing off the blindfold until he told me to.

It didn't take him long and he was soon whispering to me okay, "Okay... now" I lifted my hands the knot behind my head and untied it as fast as I could. Once the knot slid undone I pulled the material away from my eyes and gasped as tears threatened to fill my eyes.

We were standing in a slightly circular bared area surrounded by spindly bushes. Ray, however, had strung out hundreds of white fairy lights throughout the bushes around us making it seems as though we were lost in the middle of the starry sky itself. He'd laid out small tea light candles around the edges as well just to continue the romantic ambiance. In the middle of the circular sandy patch was a large red and black plaid picnic blanket with big soft pillows thrown around the edges of it and a picnic basket with a bottle of wine peeking out from under the flap of the tweed basket.

I turned to him, utterly speechless and noticed he was staring at me in anxiousness. I could imagine that someone like Ray wouldn't need to do the whole romantic gesture ordeal to get a girl and this whole thing didn't fit his tough commanding image. Which made it feel even more special that he went ahead to do this for me anyway.

"Ray... this is beautiful!" I whispered, my voice being a little croaky. "But... why? Why did you do this? You didn't need to"

I was still a little overwhelmed. No one had ever done something like this for me and I felt a little fluttering in the middle of my stomach. "You deserve this, Beauty. You deserve romantic gestures and candle lit moments. I didn't want to jump you as though you were some woman I wanted to screw and leave. " He looked deep into my eyes and in the flittering glow of the candles and the fairy lights his eyes seemed to contain every shade of brown instead of just one. "I want you, Seychelles. I know we've only known each other for a short while but there's just this... this chemistry we have and I can't ignore it"

The butterflies fluttering in my stomach began to fly in excited circles and I strode over to Ray, grabbing him by the front of his shirt and pulled him down catching him in surprise. Our lips connected and I bit his bottom lip hard enough to make him growl sexily. "You didn't need to do this Ray. I wanted you last night too. Hell, I want you still!"

He kissed me back hard and ripped our lips apart breathing heavily, his eyes dilated and screaming of his lust. It honestly made me feel so powerful. "That's just the thing Beauty. I don't sleep with women I'm not dating"

Damn, his mom taught him well. "So what are you saying, Beast?" I whispered softly.

He didn't speak at first. Instead he took my hand and pulled us over to the blanket and pressed me down against the pillows. He laid down next to me but rolled over so that he was half lying on top of me with our chests pressed together.

Ray lifted a finger and stroked the side of my jaw, pushing a tendril of hair behind my ear before holding onto my chin and making sure our eyes never left the other. "I want you to be my woman, Seychelles"

As soon as the sentence left his lips I felt all tingly inside and as actually a little light headed, like I just won the lotto. "Are you sure, Ray?" I asked uncertainly. "I don't know, I mean you deserve someone so much better and you don't even need to date me to... you know... and-" He placed his finger over my rambling lips and I blushed.

"You're going to make this difficult aren't you?" He smirked with amusement.

I sighed and shook my head. "I'm not being difficult Ray. But this just seems so surreal... I mean, we barely know each other and if you only want to date me to sleep with me, I'll sleep with you without trapping you in a relationship-" I was rambling again and this time Ray stopped it by kissing me.

His firm lips teased mine while his tongue drove me crazy. He pushed his tongue past mine and together our tongues danced an intimate tango. It wasn't just our lips he was teasing me with, no, his hands were slowly sliding down my neck. A finger traced over my collarbone from the outside towards the dip in the middle and continued to trace down over the material of my dress to the valley between my breasts.

My n!pples were standing up to attention, begging to be touched by Ray and yet he took his time as he continued his assault on my lips. The same finger smoothed over the swell of my breast and headed towards the rosy centre but instead of touching me directly he circled his finger around and around my peak. My back was arching towards him. I was unconsciously begging for him to touch me harder to move his finger just that little bit more to the centre and yet he kept pulling away so that his touch stayed soft and gentle. Against my hip, his very, very hard er*ction was throbbing and yet he did nothing to suggest he was affected by that beast of an appendage.

He pulled his lips from mine, still barely touching mine making the air I breathe only the air he was sharing with me. "Say yes, Seychelles. Say you'll be my woman" Even though his lips had stopped, his finger continued to circle around my straining n!pple and I could barely think. I was dizzy and lightheaded from so much pleasure and I wasn't entirely sure I could actually speak! He moved his mouth to my ear and toyed with my earlobe as he continued to whisper, "Say yes, baby. Be mine. Be mine, Seychelles"

His finger stroked over my n!pple as his thumb joined and he pinched it through the material of my dress while he bit my earlobe at the same time. "Say yes, baby!" He growled sexily in my ear and I was done for.

"Yes!" I squeaked.

He moved quickly and hovered over me as he ground his manhood against my core. My dress bunched up higher and higher until it gathered at my hips and the only things between us were my panties and his pants. I couldn't have hated clothes as much as I did at that moment. It didn't seem to deter him however, because he continued to ground heavily against my panties while he dipped his head to suck at the sensitive spot below my ear.

I was writhing and wriggling under him but he was too big, too heavy for me to move too much. The thrusts made the material between us rub deliciously against me and I trailed my hands up underneath his shirt feeling the smooth skin at his shoulders. His thrusts become harder and faster while he continued kissing my jaw and down my neck and pinching my nipple.

I felt my toes curl and my muscles clench tight as I screamed and exploded and pure pleasure wracked my entire body. "Sh!t" I heard Ray growl before pulling away and clenching his eyes tight. He was breathing hard but was trying to slow it down with deep breaths.

"Are you alright Ray?" I wondered out loud.

"Yeah... I'm great Beauty" He smiled. "I just wasn't expecting to do that and uh... didn't want my pants if you get what I mean" He chuckled lightly.

I bit my lip and trailed my eyes down to his still throbbing er*ction under his beige pants. "I can take care of you, you know" I suddenly felt courageous out of nowhere and stroked the tent in his lap. "But um... you'll have to teach me how"

He lifted his head and stared at me with confusion, "What do you mean?"

Although my hand lightly stroked over the material of his pants my courage disappeared as quickly as it appeared and I blushed profusely, "Um... well, I'm a virgin".

Chapter 14

I bit my lip as a furious and blazing blush heated my face and crept down my neck. Why, oh why did I have to blurt that out? Ray had been so romantic and attentive and sweet! A guy of his stature, confidence and looks wouldn't want a twenty-six year old virgin like me. I had no idea what made me spew that little confession out but my mind was buzzing with all the rejections or laughter that would come from him.

I frowned and closed my eyes not wanting to see the rejection in his eyes. Surely a man like Ray 'Beast' Hodges would want a woman who knew all the tricks to make a man feel good. I was usually a tough woman. I made it this far in my life taking care of myself and getting what I wanted, but somehow feeling as though I wasn't enough for Ray really hit a nerve. I waited, and waited for his reaction to my confession but it never came. Maybe he left already? came the unsure voice in my head.

I twitched when I felt his warm index finger and thumb hold my chin firmly and moved it to, probably, face him while I kept my eyes shut. "Open your eyes Seychelles" He whispered. His breath warmed my face and I hesitantly pried my eyes opened. I was shocked to see not a single trace of disgust or humour in his eyes. "Seychelles, you clammed up on me. What's wrong?"

His hand fell away from my chin but moved up to trace my cheekbone. "It's embarrassing…" I whispered. "I mean, I'm a virgin Ray. Someone like you would want someone better, someone more experienced. I'm just too different" He looked a little confused and slowly shook his head.

"Seychelles, your virginity is precious. You wanted to give it to me and I couldn't be more honoured. But you're right, you are different. But that's because you're precious and special as well. I'm glad you didn't just throw away something so valuable because it means you have your head screwed on right" He leaned forward and brushed his lips against mine, just the lightest caress that made my stomach bubble with anticipation and need.

"So, what now?" I wondered out loud.

He smiled and planted butterfly kisses over my forehead, eyelids, nose, cheeks chin and then lips before peppering them down my neck. He was winding me up again and he knew it. "Now… now we eat and drink some wine"

My eyes widened while my eyebrows furrowed together. What? "What do you mean? Aren't we going to-… I mean, I thought I was going to-…"

He chuckled lightly and nipped my collarbone. "Don't worry, if you still want to then we definitely will. But I will not be crude and just f*ck you as if you were another woman, Beauty" He moved up to kiss the tip of my nose, "You deserve to be made love to your first time, not f*cked, and I do recall you asking me to teach you. So I think I'll take my sweet time to get you adjusted to all your new sexual experiences"

He suddenly cupped the back of my head and pulled my lips to him as he devoured any insecurities that tried to wriggle into my mind, God he has a mouth to die for. His kiss was a promise. A promise for pleasure to come, pun intended I guess, and a promise to give as many earth shattering climaxes as I would eventually give him. I shuddered in eagerness as I moaned into his mouth and tasted the sweet taste of my Beast.

Ray's POV

Seychelles was intoxicating. I'd always prided myself in having strong will power, especially having to force it back at the base, but with this woman she just seemed like a sucker punch to the diaphragm because she always seemed to render me breathless. From her kisses I'd never guessed she was inexperienced. Her tongue and lips just moulded to mine as though they were meant for each other and when she told me she was a virgin I was more than a little surprised.

To be honest, it didn't bother me in the slightest. As a matter of fact it probably turned me on more and made me want to push into her tight little virgin body even more. The knowledge she was untouched and yet willing to give part of her body to me was honouring and made me feel like I was ten feet tall. That was the reason why I wanted to take my time with her and let her experience everything instead of hitting a home run, so to speak.

I pulled back from her kiss swollen lips and smiled when her eyes stayed shut. "Hungry, Beauty?" I asked her softly, not wanting to ruin the moment. Seychelles opened her eyes and I bit back my moan at the blatant desire swirling behind her emerald green eyes.

"Not for food" She replied. "Ray… please I want you, you can't just stop like this!"

"Well then how about I have an appetiser?" I smirked at her.

She lifted an eyebrow in confusion but I just chuckled and pushed her back gently against the cushions. I really wasn't hungry either and hell, if she wanted something to take the edge off then I was all for giving her that remedy. I bent down and kissed her throat as I moved my body to hover over hers. I could feel the slight quivers of her legs but her hands were steady as they stroked my back. I kissed my way down her long neck and arched her back to find the zipper at the back of her dress, when I did I slowly pulled it down enough to loosen her dress to pull down to her elbows.

She tried to pull her arms through the arm holes but I stopped her struggles, "Keep your arms down baby, it's much better when you just feel" The dress kept her arms from moving too much and was pushed down far enough so I was able to see her beautiful breasts rising and falling quickly under her strapless bra.

I lowered my head and traced the tip of my tongue over the swells of her breasts before using my thumbs to slowly pull her bra down. I flicked my eyes up to hers to see if she was okay with it and by the way her head was tilted back with her mouth fallen open in an 'O' I took that as a 'yes'. I quickly tugged it down and groaned at the dusty pink colour of her n!pples that stood erect and seemed to point directly at my mouth. I didn't waste any time and honed straight onto one n!pple as my finger moved to the other and I listened to her lustful mews as I tugged, licked and sucked from one rose peak to the other.

I continued to assault her peaks as I moved my hand down the curve of her waist and over her hip, down the outside her thigh and her knee before caressing across her leg and stroking back up the inside of her thigh. The closer my hand travelled to the apex of her thighs the warmer her body became and the louder her moans grew so that by the time I stroked the outside of her panties she was drenched and sleek through the material.

"Damn, Beauty. I could just imagine how hot and wet you are from the inside" I whispered against her hard n!pple. I stroked her against her panties, moving up and down before circling in the centre and used my body to keep her rising hips down. "Do you want me to touch you?"

"Yes!" She moaned loudly.

I brushed the wet material to the side and continued to tease her folds without a barrier and I clenched the muscles in my abdomen to stop from climaxing at just how moist she was for me. I pushed the tip of my finger in, teasing her entrance and yet still able to feel her inner walls clench greedily for more and I repeated the teasing thrusts until Seychelles arched quickly smothering my mouth with her soft breasts. "Ray! Stop teasing me!" She practically screamed.

I chuckled and plunged my finger in quickly earning me a hitched squeal from her. I pumped my finger and added another to the thrusts. She was so wet, so unbelievably slick that her juices were running down my hand and I needed to taste her. I abandoned her stiff peaks and kissed my way down her taut body until I met her sex and breathed in the heady smell of her essence.   I slowed my pumping fingers down and pressed my lips straight to her cl!t sucking the bundle of nerves as I circled my fingers inside of her.

Seychelles let out a scream of pleasure and I was loving how vocal she was. I sucked and flicked my tongue over her sex while thrusting and twirling my fingers and in no time her inner walls were clenching and pulling until they squeezed so tight I was barely moving my fingers anymore. With one last greedy suck to her cl!t Seychelles body exploded and I heard her dress rip as one of her arms broke through the material and her hand gripped my shoulder. Her nails bit into my skin while she screamed and moaned my name over and over again.

Once her body calmed down and all her muscles relaxed I slowly pulled my fingers out from her and licked up her sex once more tasting her juices before sucking them off my fingers. Seychelles was watching me with half hooded eyes and a lazy grin on her lips. I was rock solid down below however. Physically, I was anything but relaxed and I desperately wanted to kick down my pants to sink into her hot core. But I resisted. I was going to 'teach' her before we actually made love and I had half a mind to teach her everything tonight!

I pulled her panties up and kissed my way up her body again before pulling her bra up as well and zipping her dress. The material that crossed over her shoulder of her right arm had been ripped and I chuckled lightly at how hard she must've been pulling for it to rip. I laid down next to her kissed her temple. "Lesson number one" I whispered to her.

She purred and snuggled against my side, "I can't wait for lesson two or three or four... or as many lessons it takes before you actually put your chivalry aside and make love to me"

I couldn't but laugh at her eagerness. Damn, she was my perfect woman right here.

"Patience Beauty... trust me, waiting makes it so much better"

We laid together on the blanket as the glow from the fairy lights shook from the slight breeze while the majority of the candles had been blown out. "I'm actually pretty hungry now" Seychelles murmured quietly while drawing patterns on my stomach through my shirt.

"Well, nothing will taste as good as you anymore, but I'll go grab the food. You stay here" I stood up and brought the basket over, pulling the wine out first. I laid out some fruits and cheese along with some light sandwiches before pouring some wine for her.

We ate cushioned by the pillows and talked about everything and nothing. Once the food was finished I took out some chocolate éclairs and watched her eyes widen with happiness. "I love chocolate éclairs! But I haven't had one for so long!" She gushed.

"Well, isn't that a coincidence. They're my favourite too" I smiled. My smile dropped however when she opened her mouth wide and slipped the tip of the long chocolate éclair into her mouth and closed her lips around it, moaning a little. Aw damn...! I watched her repeat the same process over and over again until she finished the dessert and poked her tongue out to lick at the little traces of chocolate on her lips and fingers.

I will never think of chocolate éclairs the same again.

Her eyes moved to me and she cocked her head to the side, "You okay there?" I gulped and nodded before holding my éclair out to her.

"Want mine?" I offered it her.

She bit her lip and shrugged, "If you don't want it" If she ate it like the last one then I definitely didn't want to eat it. I'd give her every éclair I ever saw if I could watch her eat it like that again. In the back of my mind I knew I sounded weird, but I was so sex deprived that that little act was as though she was purring and sucking on something else entirely.

"You can have it" I shrugged trying to look normal. She took it with a smile and I watched her eat it all over again, like a guilty pleasure. Who knew watching someone eat could be so sexy? I watched her finish the whole thing before checking my watch and speaking again. "Actually there was another reason why I brought you here in particular"

"Oh? And what was that?" She asked licking the cream and chocolate from her fingers.

Almost as though it was a cue, the inky black sky would light up every few seconds as comets showered above us. "Tonight was supposed to be one of the most visible asteroid showers in the year. I just wanted to show you"

I curved my arm around her shoulders and pushed us back against the pillows again before covering us with a blanket as we watched little flickers of light streak across the sky before disappearing again. "Ray" she spoke quietly, never taking her eyes from the sky. "This is so beautiful and thoughtful. God you're so sweet!"

I kissed her hair, which smelled like coconuts, and continued to watch in silence. The asteroid shower lasted hours and even though sometimes nothing would show for a half hour it they would fly across again like little candle floating in the dark. I'd seen asteroid showers before, but watching this one with her by far the best one.

Seychelle's POV

Tonight was without a doubt the most amazing night in my entire existence. I have no idea what I did in the past life to deserve such gentle and romantic attention from someone as ruggedly handsome and sweet as Ray Hodges but I was ecstatic. I'd never seen an asteroid shower before and it really was breathtaking how something so far away could glide through the sky and look simply like a firefly making its way home.

Ray, although rippled with hard muscles, was actually quite a comfortable pillow and I couldn't help but snuggle closer to steal more of his heat. My body was still thrumming from its multiple climaxes and I literally felt like I was in heaven. The scents, the feelings, the sights and sounds... add to the mix that I now had a boyfriend. I sighed happily, it was paradise, absolute paradise, and I never wanted tonight to end.

I could feel myself becoming drowsy and I half wondered what time it was. I was sure we'd been lying down for hours and who knew how long Ray had been 'teaching' me... I had no clue, I was too lost in my little world of pleasure being set like fireworks. I stifled a yawn and hugged Ray closer still, if that was even possible and fought my fatigue so we didn't have to leave.

Ray was tracing his fingers down my arm and it felt so comforting that I couldn't help but close my eyes with the scent of apples and sea salt tickling my nose.

Chapter 15

The salt of the sea spray smelt a little stronger this morning. I inhaled deeply again as my dreams faded away to the back of my mind and felt the wind was even stronger. One of the holes in the wall must've gotten bigger, I thought in the back of my mind. I was too comfortable that I didn't want to move from my bed and I noticed that despite the stronger breeze my bed felt warmer. A pried one eyelid open and realised the sky was beginning to lighten yet the sun hadn't risen…

Whoa, wait…!

Both eyes shot open and I was instantly alert, all drowsiness having disappeared, and I suddenly realised I never went home last night. A light snore to my right made me snap my eyes to the Ray's sleeping form and I bit my lip at the slight dribble mark from the corner of his mouth. Wow… so I literally slept with Ray last night, but didn't 'make love'. That was something I hadn't expected to do when I left my house last night. Once my heart settled down and began its regular rhythm I snuggled back against Ray's warm body and felt that his arm was lazily draped over my waist.

I let my mind wonder as I watched the sky lighten to lavender, tinged with ocean blue. I'd never really been held like this before in my life. It wasn't sexual at all and yet I felt so close to Ray. Ray. God, what have I gotten myself into? Ray was planning to leave town to go back to the Air Force and yet here I am, his girlfriend, with no plans to leave because well, why should I? I spent years studying and working while trying to get my gym up and running and now I have it. I can't leave it.

A small voice in the back of my mind nagged at me, Well it's not as though Ray was asking you to move away or join the Air Force anyway. I half wondered why he even did bother to ask me to be his girlfriend. To sleep with me? It seemed a little cruel to do that if that was the case, I was freely offering him my body last night like a buffet meal to the homeless. Yet he didn't go as far as pleasuring me, not even bothering to gain pleasure for himself.

Ray was confusing and mysterious. He seemed to have many different facets to his personality and so far I'd seen a few: his knight in shining armour side, sweet and romantic side, scary Air Force brute side, mommy's boy side, handy-man side... and who knew what other side I was missing. I shook myself out from my daydream and gazed down at the beast of the man hugging me to him. God, but he was a sight for sore eyes in the morning.

He looked younger when he slept, carefree even. I leaned forward and pressed my lips against his. He stirred immediately and cupped the back of my neck to keep me there while he sucked my lower lip into his mouth and bit it so softly my eyes nearly rolled to the back of my head in bliss. His moans were gruff from sleep and I found that sound even sexier! It sounded like pure raw satisfaction and it made the butterflies wake up inside my stomach.

He kissed me once, then twice, and then once more before pulling back and smiling at me as he stroked the side of my face with the back of his fingers. "That was by far the best wake up I've gotten my beautiful girlfriend"

I blushed and rolled my eyes. "Shut up" I retorted, but my smile made him know I was joking. I didn't really know how to act, so I just tried to act as though waking up in his arms out under the brightening sky was nothing interesting.

It was pretty hard to act that way.

The battery powered fairy lights had long ago died out and the candles were slightly covered in sand already. It was actually really comforting to wake up in the middle of beach bushes and reeds under the open sky and comforted by soft sand, a blanket and a warm man by my side. I definitely could get used to this. Yeah, but for how long? Ray's not going to be staying here forever.

"What are you thinking about beautiful?" Ray asked, his voice croaky from sleep.

"Just how perfect last night and this morning is" I smiled. I stood up and stretched my arms above my head as a yawn ripped its way out of my mouth. "Want to go for a swim-ah!"

I barely finished my sentence when Ray was already up and throwing me over his shoulder as though I weighed nothing heavier than a doll and started jogging down the sandy path towards the beach. I squealed and laughed while playfully hitting his back but in all honesty I quite liked this position and the view that came with it. Ray had the ass of a God! I bit my lip and just as we pushed through the edge of the bushes I slapped his behind which made him jump a little.

"Did you just slap me?" He laughed loudly, no longer sounding tired. Hello 'playful Ray'!

"Me? No, of course not" I fluttered my eyelashes but it was useless considering he couldn't even see my face. I felt a confusingly erotic and painful slap to my own ass and squealed loudly but Ray just kept his hand there and caressed it before I heard the lapping of water getting closer.

"I recall you saying something about swimming...?" I could practically hear him grinning and the next thing I knew he was spinning us around in a circle and fell into the water. I was in no way ready to fall into the water and the cold liquid rushed up my nose I pulled out of the water laughing but spluttering as Ray doubled over in laughter at my shocked face.

"Why you...!" I stuttered. I ran through the water and tackled Ray, which was no easy feat, making the two of us fall in again and started a splashing war.

Tom's eyes slid over me again before roaming back to Ray as we sat at the counter of Sandy's kitchen. A cheeky grin grew on his lips before pointing between the two of us. "You two got it on! Shell is practically oozing sexual pleasure"

Oh geez... If I had one wish it would be to either sink into the ground at this very moment or have Tom's mouth magically disappear. My skin prickled from the blush that spread over my face and down my neck while Ray's eyes widened and darted down the hall to make sure Sandy wasn't within hearing distance. When he was satisfied that she wasn't he reached over and slapped the back of Tom's head with a loud whack.

"Ah!!! What was that for?!" Tom melodramatically shrieked.

"We didn't... uh-" I was mumbling and really didn't know how to speak at the moment.

"Firstly, what happens between me and Seychelles is none of your business Shaw. Secondly, we did not 'get it on'" Ray grumbled, looking very much as though he wanted to smack the back of Tom's head again.

Ignoring Ray's silent threat to stay silent Tom squinted his eyes as he stared at me. I squirmed under his gaze and really wished I hadn't accepted Ray's invitation to come back to his place. "Hmm, maybe 'got it on' was the wrong term... but something naughty happened between you and I like it! My spidey senses are tingling"

Ray shot him a deadpanned look, "You have spidey senses for people who hook up?"

"So something DID happen!" Tom smiled gleefully, "And yes, I happen to have hooking up spidey senses"

"Well, maybe to put you to ease Seychelles and I are dating, we're not just hooking up. You know I don't do that Shaw"

Tom's eyes widened and a Cheshire grin plastered onto his face. "Ray's already promised me the role of god father!"

Kill me now...

"I'm going to be a grandma?!" Sandy's excited voice came from my right. She was glowing and her eyes were wide with excited as she held her hands together and practically bounced with happiness.

No… kill me now, now would be a great time to kill me.

I sat at the counter with wide, shocked eyes and barely able to move. I shrank into myself, trying to become as small as I could while Ray groaned as he banged his head against the counter. "I'm so sorry Shell" He apologised, "Shaw! I will beat you so hard you won't need that flight back to the base if you don't shut up and mom, no, you are not becoming a grandma"

I peeked from between my fingers and saw both Tom and Sandy's faces drop. "Oh dear, I'm so sorry dear, I just got little excited" Sandy apologised meekly. Tom on the other hand just sulked, though I think he was just joking around.

"Come on Seychelles, I'm going to take you out for breakfast" Ray jumped off his chair and held a hand out for me so I could slide off mine too.

"Aw I'm sorry! I didn't mean it! Not really anyway" Tom groaned.

"You don't need to leave!"Ray's mom pushed.

"There is no way I'm keeping Seychelles around here at the moment, mom. She's been embarrassed enough, maybe another time if everyone behaves themselves" He shot a look at Tom but it was clear to see that everyone was forgiven. I'm sure I'll be laughing about this moment when I don't feel like digging myself to the other side of the world.

"Tom I'll see you later at the gym, I'll pick you up. Bye mom" He walked over and kissed Sandy on the cheek and she blew a kiss to me before Ray hastily pulled me outside.

"Beauty… I am so sorry! I will completely understand if you regret agreeing to date me" Ray was blushing scarlet from the scene inside and I couldn't help but laugh. For some reason he thought it was all his fault and I pulled his arm softly to stop him from walking and stood on my toes to kiss him on his chin.

"Calm down Beast. It's fine. I'll forgive you if you buy breakfast" I winked.

"Well then I better hurry up and buy you breakfast" He whispered as he smiled my favourite smile making his dimples pop out.

"Beast! I still say I'm godfather!" Tom shouted from the house while sticking his head out the window. I could also hear the light laughter from Sandy coming from inside.

Ray grumbled under his breath and helped me into the car, "If I get back into the Air Force he's going to become target practice"

Ray and I sat at outside a small cafe that I recommended. He'd been away for so long and even though he'd been back for a few months he hadn't really gone exploring the restaurants and cafes. Shoreside Cafe was one of my favourite cafes to eat at when I was able to eat out. It wasn't as popular as the others or as big, but the food was generous and cheap as well as delicious.

Ray had ordered the big breakfast, no surprise there, and I'd ordered the buttermilk pancakes with bacon on the side. After our swim this morning we walked to my house so I could shower and change into denim shorts and a baggy t-shirt while I offered Ray a dry towel. We went back to our hidden picnic spot and collected everything before walking to his house where he showered and changed, and where I almost died of embarrassment.

"So... regret being my girlfriend yet?"

I rolled my eyes and they landed on Ray who was watching me carefully. "Calm down, boyfriend, embarrassing families are a part of the deal too aren't they? You got lucky seeing as mine aren't alive anymore, so I guess Tom kind of has a reason to be double as embarrassing" I grinned. His smile wasn't as big as I hoped it to be and I cocked my head to the side. "What's wrong?"

"You don't seem bothered by the fact that your family's not alive. What happened to them if you don't mind me asking..."

I stayed silent for a while. Talking about my dad was always a hard topic to talk about. Ray let me have a moment to myself while I breathed deeply before looking back up to him. "I was brought up by my dad. It was pretty much the two of us from what I could remember. He was an only child and his parents had him while they were already old so I never met my grandparents either. My house... It was built by my great grandad on his dad's side and it was always just passed down through the generations. The reason it was left to me was because my dad was smart enough to have his will drawn up. He passed away when I was eighteen and I've pretty much been independent since then"

I shrugged my shoulders as I told my quick life story and skipped any actual details. I still had nights when I laid in bed and cried at the memory of my dad wincing in pain even through the strong medication and pain killers. I wasn't sure if I was ready to share that quite yet even though it had been eight years. I blinked rapidly and cleared my throat to try to get rid of my discomfort. "How about your mom?" I could tell Ray was curious, after all we'd already decided to date but didn't really know anything about each other.

"Oh... I never knew her. I went through a phase in my early teens when I wanted to know my mom and always asked my dad questions but from what I learnt I sort of wished he never told me. Apparently my mom never wanted me. She only kept me because my dad begged her not to abort me. Apparently I was a tough pregnancy and he ended up telling her to stop working, for her and my own sake, and he would take care of everything, which he did. She went into early labour but was only thirty-five weeks pregnant so the doctors pushed ahead and I was barely the size of a ruler. I weighed three pounds and was in special care for a month before I was discharged. My mother, however, left without a trace after she was discharged"

"What?!" Ray's eyes were as round as dinner plates and his jaw slackened as it hung open.

I shrugged my shoulders. I didn't talk about my mom because I didn't want the pity but it didn't bother me. I had no feelings towards the runaway mother who wouldn't have loved me anyway. Her leaving turned out for the better. "That's what I understood from the bits and pieces my dad told me and a whole lot of digging through my hospital paperwork. It's okay though, I ended up in the care of my dad and he loved me more than his own life. So yeah... you're very lucky Ray. Sandy is an amazing mom"

He offered me a sad smile at first but at the mention of his mom and the sadness melted away to pride. "Yes, I'm very lucky to have my mom. I'm sorry about yours though Beauty"

I waved my hand to dismiss the apology. "There's no need. She was a pathetic excuse of a mother and the only thing I have to thank her for is not killing me in her womb"

The serious conversation was halted when our orders were brought out to us by the kind, big bellied owner, Billy. "Brought a friend along I see Shell" He smiled happily. His cheeks were full and he sort of reminded me of a bald and beardless Santa. "You treat her right, boy, or you'll have me to speak to"

Billy's threatening face was hilarious because the man could not seem to pull any other face besides a happy smiling one, and the fact that he called Ray 'boy' was laughable. Ray was anything but a 'boy'. Nonetheless, Ray humoured him and nodded seriously. "Yes, sir. I don't plan on hurting Seychelles at all. By the way, the food looks amazing"

Always the gentleman and charmer.

Billy winked over at me and I couldn't help but giggle. He put down my usual extra maple syrup and left us to eat. Ray was already digging in and moaning in delight at the food. His plate was overflowing with toast, sausages, bacon, tomato with cheese, eggs and beans. I had a suspicion that Billy added more food considering just how big a man Ray was. I picked up the maple syrup and drizzled it over the pancakes and bacon and began to eat.

"Did you just put syrup on your bacon, Beauty?" Ray was cocking an eyebrow as though I'd lost my mind.

I nodded and mumbled a yes through my food before swallowing. "Of course! Haven't you ever tried it?" He shook his head with a chuckle. "I accidently drenched my bacon with maple syrup when I was younger and never looked back. Honestly, it's so good. Here, try some"

I speared a piece of bacon dripping with syrup and held it up to his mouth. He happily ate the piece and gave a surprised moan. "You're right, that's really good. Sweet and salty"

I chuckled and continued to eat, happy that the serious conversation about my parents was over and he didn't catch on that I never actually gave details besides about my mom. Honestly, I felt nothing for the woman who walked out on me without a second glance. Talking about her and what little participation she had in my life was like reading black text on yellowing paper. It was just a paragraph of my life and nothing more. Of course I would've loved to have a mother who cared and showed me into womanhood by good example but... it didn't matter anymore.

"I have to say... after my mom's cooking, this food is the best I've tasted!" Ray complimented breaking me out of my inner monologue.

I laughed and finished off my pancakes. "That was such a mommy's boy comment, 'Beast'"

The sun was shining brightly and as it shifted slowly across the sky the shadow of umbrella shading us moved slightly allowing me to close my eyes and bask in the sunshine. "Hey Shell, nice to see you outside of the gym"

I opened my eyes and saw Cole Richards, one of my regular members at the gym and long time friend. He was tall, obviously not as tall as Ray, and muscular, though once again not as much as Ray. I'd known him for almost ten years now and he's always been there when I needed someone, even when he knew I preferred my alone time.

"Cole! Wow what a surprise. I don't normally see you out and about. It's been a while" Cole was a good looking guy, he always had been. His cocoa coloured skin seemed to always be flawless ever since I met him and his soft brown eyes were always smiling. His brown hair was cut down to a buzz cut and he looked as though he just came from the beach, if his board shorts and bare torso was anything to say. And his wash board abs really didn't need much else to say. "Oh, Cole this is Ray my boyfriend, Ray this is Cole. He and I've been friends for years now"

Ray eyed Cole as Cole did the same and I seemed to be missing some sort silent conversation as they shook hands. "Boyfriend huh, Shell? That's a first" Cole sounded surprised. His smiled but something looked a little off about it, as if it didn't seem to reach his eyes like it normally does.

I blushed. Cole would know, he would playfully tease me that he'd always warn the other guys off because no one would be good enough for me. "Yeah, well Ray was worth the long wait"

Ray gave me his dimpled smile and kissed the back of my hand. It spoke more than words so it was fitting that he simply held my hand while looking into my eyes with a smile. "So it seems. You guys look like a great couple. We should all get together some time, maybe hit up the clubs for old time sake"

I scrunched my nose. I never really was one for clubbing for it seemed like a good idea to get my boyfriend and my old friend to get to know each other. I looked at Ray and saw him shrugging, "If Beauty wants to then I'm happy to go"

Cole raised his eyebrow at the nickname and I suddenly felt the pressure of going to the clubs. "Sure, why not. Friday night sound alright?" Cole and Ray nodded before Cole had to go and with a goodbye to me and another handshake with Ray he carried his surf board and strolled across the street.

Chapter 16

"Why is it not surprising that Tom is flirting with my gym members?" I laughed as Ray and I walked into my gym.

I watched in amusement as Tom increased the speed and inclination of the treadmill he was practically sprinting on as he grinned at the woman running on the treadmill next to him. Tom was a good looking guy. While, at first glance, the most domineering feature of Ray was his build and how sturdy he was, Tom's domineering feature was his charismatic personality. It practically oozed off him as though he perspired charm instead of sweat and the woman on the treadmill was falling for it hook, line and sinker.

I was actually quite intrigued to see how this would turn out, so Ray and I stood to the side as we watched Tom run faster which only resulted in him sweating more and his defined muscles bulge as his arms swung back and forth. The woman's eyes were flickered from the screen in front of her to Tom's body and as soon as she looked up at his face he winked and smiled. That small gesture was enough to make the woman lose her footing on the treadmill and sent her flying back against the wall behind her.

My eyes widened and I was already starting to take a step forward to see if she okay when Tom caught me by surprise and purposely copied her. His fall was obviously premeditated as he was sent hurtling down against the wall next to her, effectively taking away some of the embarrassment from her. He landed with an 'oomph!' but looked over at her breathing hard and sent her a crooked smile. "So... come here often?"

I stuffed my fist in my mouth as I burst out laughing. I was practically choking on my laughter at how seriously he asked her without so much as a hint of embarrassment that they're sprawled on the floor against a wall with their treadmills still whirring. "Smooth, isn't he?" Ray chuckled shaking his head.

"I have to give him credit" I laughed wiping a tear from my eye as random shudders of laughter wracked my shoulders. "He's good. I'm so glad he doesn't affect me... that fall looked painful"

That made Ray finally burst out in laughter and he kissed the top of my head. His laughter caught Tom's attention as he looked up to see us with a cheeky grin. He stood up and helped the woman up as well, but before walking over to us he flipped her hand over and kissed the back of it.

Smooth.

"Well, if it isn't the love birds! How's my godson or goddaughter coming along?" My smile dropped and I shot him a dead panned face before looking over to a blushing Ray who was glaring at his best friend.

"Shaw... my leg may have been shot and is recovering... but there is nothing wrong with my fists" He warned Tom. Tom raised his hands in defence but his smirk showed he was holding another comment back.

I simply watched them with an amused grin playing on my lips. "Boys, boys we have work to do" I playfully chastised them.

"Oh, already getting told off by the girlfriend. Looks like the Beauty has put the Beast on a leash" Tom laughed before making whipping noises. I rolled my eyes and Ray grumbled under his breath. Where does Tom seriously get these comments?

"You ready Ray?" I asked throwing my baggy tank top into my office so I stood in a sports bra, leggings and running shoes.

"Always" He replied stretching out his arms across his body.

I could tell that even though Ray was fit now, he used be even more fit before his injury. Having had to stay in shape for such a long period of time his muscle memory would help a lot to get him back into the same fitness level or maybe even better within a shorter time period. I instructed him and helped him throughout his training and most of the time he didn't need it. I just liked hovering about him. Tom, who had 'helped' at the beginning, was now back to flirting with another woman seeing as the first one had already left. Probably from a bruised tailbone... and dignity.

"How's your leg feeling?" I asked as I watched Ray holding a barbell across his broad shoulders and slowly doing squats. I had insisted that he do these at the end before warming down on the treadmill because it would help his thighs, especially his shot thigh, and I could tell it was still bothering him once he began to stand back up. Plus the sight of his buns of steel was swoon worthy.

"It's getting better" He panted out, "Right now, yeah, it's hurting but only because you're trying to kill me with these slow squats"

I laughed and counted down his last squat before pulling it to the side onto the metal shelf. "Stop being a baby, it's not that bad. Okay, ten minutes on the treadmill on a fast jog before walking for five minutes then you're donc"

He ran the fifteen minutes and by the time he stepped off I threw a cold water bottle at him and watched him gulp it down like a dying man in a desert. "You'd probably do better than a lot of other woman, and men, back in the military" He said after finishing the water. "You seem have no end to your endurance. I have good stamina... but damn, I might have to work on it to keep up with you"

I did a double take at Ray when his words registered into my brain. There was so much double meaning to that simple sentence and I found myself blushing at my dirty thoughts of us matching our stamina together. Damn.

"I'm going to hit the showers. I'll pick you up tonight?"

I nodded, "Yeah, sounds great. Come around, say nine o'clock, and we'll grab something to eat before going into town" He nodded in reply and winked before heading into the men's locker room.

I decided to get in a bit of training in myself seeing as I planned on drinking a little tonight and headed over to my office to grab my ipod before hopping onto a treadmill and running to my 'Running' album full of fast paced songs that pumped me up and kept up with my thundering heat beats.

Once again I was stumped on what to wear. Clubbing? I hadn't gone clubbing in what seemed like years and had no idea what the women were wearing to the clubs nowadays. Ray had called before my shower apologising as he asked if Tom could come along as well. In the background I could hear Tom begging for me to say 'yes' and I couldn't stop the fit of giggles that threatened to suffocate me. I'd told them that Tom was more than welcome to come along and Ray had thanked me though it was a cute mixture of relief and annoyance at Tom.

I'd braided my hair in thick braids after my shower and added a few spritz of sea salt mixed with water and gel over it while I was back to staring my closet. I really needed a new wardrobe but since shopping for clothes wasn't really something I enjoyed I, once again, made do with what I had. I paired a khaki tube top that had cute golden buttons, which sort of reminded me of the military, with a simple high waisted black skirt. A thin belt would've gone nicely with the outfit, but seeing as I didn't own one, I shrugged and added my only pair of black wedge heels that matched anything and was about as formal as I went.

I stared at my reflection and thought, oh, why the hell not, before adding mascara, and eye liner and slapping my cheeks for colour. I didn't own any fancy lipsticks or eye shadows so I simply swiped on my lip balm and took out my braids letting my, now, wavy hair fall down my back in stylish beach waves.

Simple and not-so-casual, that was me at my most dressed up.

I was reconsidering my top when I heard a knock against the door and I realised it was already nine o'clock. "Coming!" I shouted in the direction of the door as I rushed around my room grabbing my lip balm, phone, keys and tossing anything I might need from my wallet into a plain black clutch with a thick strap for my wrist.

I yanked my door open to see Ray looking down. His eyes took in my heeled feet and slowly grazed up my legs and up the curves of my body. By the time his eyes reached mine my cheeks were flushed and I felt as though he'd just completely undressed me with just his eyes. "You, Seychelles, are one beautiful woman" He breathed.

I bit my lip and tore my eyes from his gaze. They were just so penetrating. Instead I took in what he was wearing. He wore fitted, dark jeans and a black button down shirt with boots encasing his feet. He looked positively edible. "And you, Ray, make me one lucky woman" I didn't miss the slight blush colouring his cheekbones.

"Come on! You have all night to stare at each other! I'm starving!" Tom yelled from the back seat. Tom seemed to be the epitome of 'mood killer' today and my poor eye sockets were getting a good work out from all the eye rolling I seemed to be doing today.

"I'm so sorry" Ray apologised with a shake of his head.

"There's no need to apologise Ray honestly, it's okay. I'm happy Tom's coming along" I was pretty sure I was happy anyway.

I hopped into the front seat and greeted Tom who winked and had his ever present grin on his face. Ray drove us to a small Chinese restaurant that was overly decorated and smelt heavenly. The food was amazing and by the end of the meal all three of us were fighting over who was going to pay for the bill. I had been shut down for paying it by the two men and watching them like a tennis match over who was going to pay.

"Let's just leave" Tom said.

"What... without paying?" Ray looked at him in confusion.

A waitress smiled as she reached our table and gave a card to Tom who was grinning from ear to ear. "I gave my card about half way through the meal and told them to pay the bill with it when we finished" He laughed popping his card back into his wallet.

My jaw dropped before I burst in laughter and was joined by Ray. "Why the hell were we arguing then?!" Tom shrugged.

"Gave us something to do, I guess"

I was in high spirits and by the time we walked up to the club and the line was long full of younger men and women. I walked right up to the bouncer with a smile, "Hey Carl, how's that torn tendon treating you? I haven't seen you in a while at the gym"

Carl was another frequent member at the gym and well, I might as well use my connections to get inside faster. "Getting better every day, Shell. I'll probably get back to the gym in another few weeks. You heading in tonight?"

"Yep, we should there under Cole's name" Carl nodded, already knowing Cole from the gym, and scanned his clipboard and nodded while crossing names off.

"Head on in"

"Take it easy, Carl!"

"Wow, your woman's got connections, Beast. I like it!" Tom hollered.

As soon as we stepped inside the bass and music boomed in my ears. I was so used to the quiet whooshing of wind and splashing of the ocean waves that this was a shock to my system. I looked back and noticed Tom was already in flirt mode and heading off. Looks like he's happily taking care of himself, I noted with a smile.

Apparently tonight was an old R'n'B night and the songs playing hit me in just the right way. The DJs played songs that just made everyone want to grab the person closest to them and dance dirty with them. There was just something about the era of these songs that made me feel so young and carefree and I could feel any bit of apprehension disappear as we squeezed deeper inside the thudding club.

Ray was yelling to me but the music drowned out so he acted out if I wanted a drink. I nodded and he slipped a possessive arm around my waist as we danced our way through the throng of people. The body heat of everyone was beginning to make my skin slick with sweat so that by the time we reached the bar a drink was very much needed already. I shouted at the bartender for a rum and coke and Ray asked for the same. As our drinks were being made I swung my hips from side to side letting the music thump through my body. I hadn't really danced in a long time and it left my hips feeling a little stiff.

I looked through the people wondering where Cole could be. I recognised probably only half the people here which only made it harder to try and find him. Something cold was held against the side of my neck and I jumped realising that Ray had our drinks, he offered me mine and leaned forward so that his lips were brushing against the shell of my ear, "To letting loose and feeling free"

I repeated his toast and together we pulled our heads back and drank it all in one long gulp. His eyes were hypnotising and suddenly I felt courageous as the alcohol burnt through my system. I kept our eyes connected as I held his hand and pulled him towards the dance floor. As I walked, I swung my hips from side to side to the beat of the song. All of a sudden the song changed and it sounded so sexual I couldn't help but line my back to the front of his body. I began rolling my body as I grinded my ass back to him and he didn't hesitate to grip my hips as he began to dance along with me.

Our bodies moved in sync as heat enveloped us and I couldn't help but think of another way that we could be moving in sync. Ray pulled me harder back against him and I gasped at the hardness that pressed against me. I tipped my head back and raised my arm up to wrap around his neck behind me which brought us even closer together. We danced for several songs, all sounding sexy and perfect for me to rub my body against Ray's.

"Hey Shell! Glad you could make it!" The sound of Cole's happy voice snapped me out of my sexual dream of being wrapped up with nothing but Ray around me. His smile was contagious and I grinned back thanking him for inviting us. "No problem! Ray, nice seeing you again!"

The two men shook hands but I noticed Ray kept one hand gripped to my hipbone and would squeeze them every once in a while which set off little jolts of pleasure straight to my core. We walked off the dance floor and to a booth Cole had hired for the night. "Will you be alright for a few minutes Seychelles?" Ray asked me intently.

"Yeah, of course. What's wrong?"

"I saw Tom back there and let's just say he doesn't always realise when a woman is taken. I just need to make sure he's not drunk off his face and looking at a broken nose any time soon. He chuckled and I shooed him off to look for his friend.

"Where's your friend going?" Cole asked handing me a rum and coke.

"Boyfriend. And he's looking for his friend in case his friend gets on the wrong side some woman's jealous boyfriend" I laughed taking a sip from the cool glass. "I'm really surprised you managed to find us in here Cole, the place is packed!"

"Yeah, I guess. But I noticed you easily enough. After ten years I'm pretty sure I can recognise those legs of yours. You may be short Shell, but you're pretty much all legs" I burst out laughing and half wondered why. It wasn't really that funny but I guessed it had something to do with the alcohol. I never was one who could handle my liquor well.

"Well, I looked out for you and couldn't see squat!" I finished off my drink and continued swaying to the music while I gazed round the club.

The girls, I noticed, wore much shorter skirts, shorts and dresses than I was and were much more revealing in their choice of clothing. It made me painfully aware how plain I actually dressed when I noticed how glittery, shiny and tight they all dressed with matching jewellery and sky high pumps with immaculate make up. I completely passed on wearing any sort of jewellery, even earrings, and my clothing began to look more like something they'd wear to the mall rather than out clubbing.

Cole finished his drink and pointed his thumb over at the dance floor again. "Want to dance? I don't see Ray anymore and it looks like you want to keep dancing" I was actually surprised at how well I was able to hear now considering the thunderous bass and music.

I looked around and realised that Ray had disappeared. I mentally shook my head, Tom really was a force to be reckoned with. "Sure, you can keep me company while Ray's looking for Tom"

He led us out to the dance floor with a hand on the small of my back and helped me push through the people when they got a little too grabby. Once we reached the floor I moved away slightly and began dancing to the beat again. Cole was a good dancer. He had the kind of body and moves where dancing came naturally for him. For any dances in high school he and I would always partner up and dance together so dancing with him now felt like old times.

I was shoved forward by some guy and flew straight into Cole's chest. He wrapped his arms around my shoulders to stop us from falling over and steadied me on my feet. "Hey!

Watch it!" He shouted at the group of men who were dancing behind me.

They turned at Cole's shouting and scoffed but as their eyes landed on me they smirked and turned to give us more attention. Cole carefully pushed me behind him shielding me from their eyes. God, where was Ray? "Well aren't you a pretty little thing" The closest guy slurred. They were all very obviously wasted if their swaying bodies and blood shot eyes had anything to say. "How 'bout a dance good lookin'?"

I cringed, "No thanks"

Cole was still eyeing them and shielding me like a human barrier but the man who had bumped into me was walking closer. "Aw come on darlin', just one dance. I bet your boyfriend here ain't great company"

Was he serious?

"He's not my boyfriend. And no, I don't want to dance with you"

The guy looked back at his friends and laughed. "She's playing hard to get! I like that! I like the chase!" Cole, I could tell even from behind him, was furious and began to walk us back to move away from the drunken group of men. "Hey, I said I want a dance!"

He no longer looked amused but looked angry now. "I believe she said 'no' man, so I'd let it drop if I were you" Cole threatened. I pulled at the back of his shirt, not wanting a fight and just to look for Ray and Tom.

"Oh look at that, the 'not boyfriend' is getting protective" He snorted. His laughter cut short when he suddenly moved forward and sloppily threw a punch at Cole in the stomach.

It was so unexpected that it winded Cole and I literally heard all the wind get knocked out of him.

Drunk Man reached forward and grabbed my wrist pulling me forward from behind Cole. "I said, I want a dance" He growled angrily.

"Fuck off!" I heard Cole shout I was being yanked back and he threw a punch at Drunk Man across his jaw.

I screamed, but it was only drowned out by the changing of the song. "Cole! Stop! Come on let's just go!"

Cole was suddenly held down three of Drunk Man's friends while Drunk Man began throwing punch after punch. "Stop! STOP!" I screamed. By now they'd gotten the attention of the people around them and instead of stopping them, people just watched while others were insane enough to pull out their phones and record the fight!

I jumped forward and tried to shove Drunk Man away but, even though I worked out regularly, he was only put off balance momentarily before back handing me across the face and going back to Cole. Pain exploded behind my cheek but I ignored it as I watched as tears fell from my eyes at what was unfolding before me.

"Seychelles!" I turned and relief filled me when I saw Ray and Tom shoulder barging their way through the crowd. "Shaw get her out! Now!"

Ray looked like he was in airman mode now. His tone was sharp and stern and even Tom's playful attitude was gone as he nodded once and pulled me away from the scuffle. "Tom! What are you doing! Let me go, you have to help Cole and Ray!"

Tom snorted, "Please Shell... Ray could probably kill all of them with one hand. I have no doubt this will be finished within a matter of minutes"

Tom dragged me through the doors and the cool air hit me like another slap to the face. He forced me to sit on the curb while he dashed into the corner store and bought me a bottle of water. He winced and held it to my cheek. With the adrenaline slowly leaving my system I began to notice the throbbing in my cheek and cringed at how hard Drunk Man actually hit me.

I stared back at the innocent looking doors and hope Ray and Cole was okay. Tom rolled his eyes, "They'll be fine. Not sure about your little friend, but Ray for sure will come out feeling a little better after he's had a few punches thrown around. Trust me!"

Chapter 17

R ay's POV

Music thumped all around us and yet I barely registered it. Green and red lights flashed across everyone's faces but once again, I barely noticed it while I stared at the drunken man who had ruined Seychelles' night. I was thankful now that Tom begged to come along to the club because if he hadn't been here to drag her away from harm then I wouldn't be standing dead centre of the club, staring daggers at the cocky drunkard.

"You'd be smart to let him go" I growled over the music to the three men holding Cole down. My blood still boiled at seeing the pathetic excuses of men standing in front of me who jumped another man trying to defend a woman. My respect grew for Cole. I was across the club but they were within my vision considering I could see above the majority of the people in here and I saw everything unravel. While I wasn't too happy about another man dancing with my woman, I was at least glad he had the decency to not grind against her and even put himself between her and these cowards.

The Drunk Man scoffed while his friends, who looked a little less drunk than him, continued to hold Cole down but began to look a little uneasy. "You're not a part of this! He made me lose my dance with that slu-"

My eye twitched when I realised where his mind was leading to and even before he could finish his sentence my fist shot out and cracked against his jaw. It was a clean hit and sent him stumbling backwards, falling into a few people behind him. Drunk Man's friends released Cole and rushed towards me as Cole slumped to the ground. Well if it was a fight they wanted. It was a fight they would get.

I rolled my shoulders back and cracked my neck from side to side while my eyes narrowed at them. Two of the men tried to jump me and hold me down, the same way they did with Cole, but I dropped down and swiped my leg down and backwards tripping them to the ground. I shoved my knee into the throat of the closest one keeping him on the ground as he clawed at my knee and gasped for air. My weight held my knee down firmly enough that even though he was pushing and shoving with everything he had, he couldn't budge me.

I was thundering down punch after punch on his other friend who had tried to jump me. His face had split in several places and gushing blood, as all head wounds would. His eye was quickly swelling shut and his once white teeth were stained red. With every jab and right hook I landed, more of his blood painted my knuckles red. I had to give it to the man, however, he definitely had heart if he could withstand this many punches. However, with one last solid jab his eyes rolled back presenting the whites of his eyes in surrender and he fell unconscious.

The booming music had conveniently switched to a song that pumped the blood in me for the fight and I dodged the foot of the third man as it came flying straight for my temple and grabbed his ankle. His eyes widened momentarily before I twisted it quickly and tugged hard sending him falling to the ground with either a dislocated or twisted ankle to join his friend; who had passed out from lack of oxygen. The fall was hard, I could even hear the thud of his head meeting the ground over the music. People had gathered around, circling us like vultures hungry for more of a fight. They cheered and hollered, pumping their fists in the air and acting like animals. I stood up, no longer needing to keep my knee down and decided to let the last of Drunk Man's friend conscious. Speaking of which...

I looked around wondering where the prick had gone to only to have my silent question answered as glass shattered over my head. I clenched my jaw and slowly turned around to see Drunk Man holding a broken bottle with jagged edges glinting under the coloured lights. My breathing had deepened and as I exhaled my hot breaths came out in growls. I dusted the shattered glass from my shoulders, ignoring the tiny stabs as the glass shards were ripped from my skin, and slowly prowled around Drunk Man in a circle.

He glanced down, taking in his two unconscious friends and one injured friend who was clasping his ankle in pain. With every slow step I took, he stepped away continuing our circling like two lions readying themselves to be the dominant winner. His jaw had grown an impressive welt and purpling slightly as the blood beneath the skin began its bruising. Every beat of my heart pumped to the bass of the music and suddenly I stopped. A smirk tugged at the corner of my lips and it was enough to send the alcohol ridden drunk to come running at me brandishing his broken bottle like a dagger.

His arm came up, his intention was clear in his blurred eyes of what he was about to do. He brought the jagged edges of the beer bottle down aiming for my face but the alcohol coursing through his blood stream slowed him down and I swiftly swerved my arm up. My forearm caught his and I pushed it farther back making him stumble again and lose his grip on the bottle. I charged at him in the short distance and grabbed him by the front of his shirt, both my fists clenching at the material of his shirt.

I lifted him higher and continued running. The crowd part-ed like the Red Sea and I shoved him hard against the column I landed against. His head lopped back and smacked painfully against the cement. I dragged him up higher and held his neck with one hand instead of his shirt before bringing my face close to his. The stench of beer was strong on him and he looked worse for wear as he struggled breathe and kicked his legs uselessly in the air.

"You fucked with the wrong man, as\$hole. If I ever see or even hear that you so much as glimpsed at my woman again I will not hesitate to show you the end of my gun" I growled softly as I stared straight into his eyes, making sure he focused on what I was saying. "Do you understand me?" He choked and wheezed as he struggled to answer me while I clenched harder around his throat. "I said, do... you... understand... me?"

"Y-yes!" He choked out, his face beginning to turn blue.

I released my hold on his throat and he fell in a crumpled heap on the ground. A tap on my shoulder made me turn around only to come face to face with one of the bouncers from the club. "As much as I'm happy that idiot won't be harassing women any time soon, I'm going to have to ask you to leave sir" He had a slight smile on his lips as he escorted me out and I had a feeling he'd been wanting to do what I did for a while.

I raised an eyebrow as we reached the exit and looked over to him. "It took you a while to stop me... not that you actually did stop me...?" I commented curiously.

The bouncer shrugged, "That guy was Lee Adams. He's always harassing the women around here and we never catch him. He's usually slicker than he was tonight and harasses the women near the bathrooms so no one sees, so by the time we find out he's already gone or no one can prove it"

"He's a f*cking prick... nothing but a waste of precious air" I murmured. "Look, my girlfriend's friend is still in there. He's the one the cowards jumped and he might need to go to the hospital. Seeing as I'm not allowed back in make sure someone calls an ambulance, yeah?" The bouncer nodded and left me outside as I began to look for Seychelles and Tom.

"Ray!" I was knocked backwards against a tree when Seychelles came hurtling out of nowhere and hugged me tightly around my waist. She was crying and sniffling while mumbling something into my shirt. "-ahndb I wasch shoew fwieb-ntd!"

I held her shoulders gently and pulled her back enough to see her face. Her face was tear stained and her nose was a little red. I ground my teeth when I saw the red mark across her cheek from where Lee Adams had hit her. Seeing her skin reddened from being hit made me want to march back inside and knock that bastard unconscious, but she sniffed and all my attention was back on her.

"I can't understand you, beautiful" I whispered. "What's wrong? Are you okay?"

"I was so frightened!" She cried hugging me tight again.

I felt my heart clench as I hugged her small body close to me, reassuring her with my own embrace. "Beauty, I'm okay. No harm down and those guys learnt a lesson..." I stopped there, figuring she didn't need to know the details.

A cough sounded from behind me, making me crane my neck. "You got a little something on your shoulders and head man" Tom pointed out.

I brushed my shoulders and noticed small cuts from the glass and again at the back of my head to see a small amount of blood from where the bottle had been broken. It barely hurt and I hadn't really even noticed it, but it didn't stop Seychelles' eyes widening in shock. "Ray! What in the world happened in there?! Are you okay! This is all my fault!"

I stopped her panicking with a chaste kiss to her lips and held her chin tightly, "I'm... fine... Seychelles" I comforted her with kisses between every word. "Relax..."

Then just like that the stiffness in her shoulders and the tenseness in her spine eased and she began kissing me back with fervour. She pressed herself hard against me and wrapped her arms around my neck as her tongue traced my lower lip. I parted my lips for her, enjoying her dominance, as she stroked my tongue with hers. Bending down, I and scooped her up so she wouldn't have to tip toe to reach me and spread my hands over her round globes, holding her against me.

Damn her kisses were insatiable.

A throat cleared behind us, "Well, not that this isn't hot or anything... but it's seriously making me feel lonely and if I don't get action soon I'm pretty sure my right hand will..."

Mood-instantly-killed.

Our lips broke apart and we both gasped for air. "Bloody hell Shaw... I don't know whether to thank you for keeping Beauty safe... or strangle you for constantly interrupting" I growled. I looked down at Seychelles and noticed her flushed cheeks and deep breathing while she tried to calm herself. "Come on Beauty, I'll drop Tom back at mine before dropping you off home"

I tugged on her hand and the three of us walked back to the car while Tom yapped on about how he missed out on the action inside. Once again Seychelles' rode shotgun and I drove in silence with the windows down. The moon was bright, whole and amber tonight while the silver stars twinkled beside it like glitter. I noticed Seychelles staring at my hands and looked down, only to cringe when I realised she was staring at the dried blood on my knuckles.

"They deserved it Beauty. No man should ever treat a woman that way, and according to the bouncer they've been at it for a while" I was defending myself. I was hoping Seychelles wouldn't think I was some sort of monster who lived for the blood of arrogant son of a bitc-

"So it's not yours?" Her small voice asked.

My eyebrows popped upwards towards my hairline in surprise. "No, it's not mine"

She sighed deeply in relief and smiled slightly. "Thank Go d... I think I keep underestimating you Beast"

I smiled and winked down at her, "That's a dangerous thing to do, Beauty"

I dropped Tom off and rolled my eyes at him when he began thrusting into the air with his thumbs up at me behind Seychelles back. Sometimes I don't even know who that guy is... The drive back to Seychelles house was silent, a comfortable silence, filled only by the roar of the car, the howling wind and crashing of the waves that were hidden behind the bushes.

I parked the car in front of her house and stepped out, walking quickly around to open the door for her. She smiled as I held her hand and shut the door for her before walking hand in hand to the front door. "You should come in for a bit" She said sternly, "I want to clean up your cuts and then wash the blood off"

I nodded and followed her inside. The wind rattled the house and I mentally reminded myself that I needed to fix any holes so wind wouldn't make it inside anymore. "How

come you've never had anyone come by to fix it the house?"
I asked curiously.

She shrugged, "Never had the extra money to, I guess"

"Well, I'll come by again to fix the holes. The roof is all fixed
but it sounds, and feels, like there are holes or cracks in the
walls that need fixing too" I nodded to myself. I wanted to
make sure Seychelles house was all fixed and in top shape.

Seychelles walked into the kitchen and pointed at the chair
by the bench. "Sit" I chuckled and sat down watching her
sassy little movements. "I'm going to grab the first aid kit
then clean you up. I'll be right back"

As Seychelles padded down the hallway to look for her first
aid kit my mind wandered to the future. Seychelles looked
good in my future… but could she fit in it? The Air Force was
my life. It literally had been for the last ten years and before
then I always wanted it to be. I never bothered to come back
home to visit my mom, as much as I loved her, I just never
came back.

Could I do the same with Seychelles? No, of course I
wouldn't. Seychelles didn't deserve a one sided relationship
and I wouldn't ever make her wait like that. I sighed and
rubbed a calloused hand over my face. So I had a choice, and
a tough one at that. Was I going to break it off with Seychelles
and return to the AF? Or retire a veteran and make a life for
us here in our hometown?

Seychelles' POV

Did tonight really just happen?

Did my boyfriend really just defend my honour?

Oh no, what happened to Cole? I growled. Too much happened tonight and ended with badass Ray coming out for a bit, not that it was entirely a bad thing, but I was hoping for seductive and funny Ray tonight. "There you are!" I whooped when I found the first aid kit under the bathroom sink.

"Were you talking to the plumbing or to me?" Ray's amused voice came from behind me. "Either way, I don't mind if you keep bending over like that. That's quite a view Beauty"

My face blushed scarlet when I realised my position; crouching on my knees and elbows since I had to look at the back of the cupboard under the sink, my behind clearly the most prominent feature at the moment. I stood up quickly but didn't have time to turn around when Ray came up behind me, his heat enveloping me as he pressed his body against mine.

"Need some help there, beautiful?" He whispered into my ear, his hot breath tickling my ear. Suddenly his large, rough hands gripped my hips and I was turned and lifted onto the vanity. He stepped forward and widened my legs so he could fit between my knees and caged me in as he planted his hands on either side of me. "I'm all ready, Doctor Beauty"

I felt instantly hot and wished I was able to clench my thighs together, but with Ray filling up the space between them it was impossible. I cleared my throat and ignored the fluttering in my stomach as I put the first aid kit to the side and grabbed some cotton and wetting it. Oh dear... "You'll uh, you'll need to take off your shirt Ray" I whispered, my voice hoarse from sexual tension.

He smirked and leaned back, momentarily offering me some space to gather my thoughts and breathe properly. However, my throat seized up when he grabbed the back of his shift and lifted it off over his head in one swift movement before throwing it to the ground.

Oh wow.

Oh wow, oh wow, oh wow.

His chest is so close. So, so close.

I could feel myself salivating at how close he was, only to realise that he was moving even closer as he returned back to his position of caging me in. "Clean away" He whispered.

I gulped and cleared my throat bringing my hand up to dab away at the spots of blood decorating his oh so very broad shoulders. I kept my eyes directly on the smooth skin of his shoulders, never straying towards his eyes that were watching me like a hawk. I frowned when I felt little sharp shards sticking in his skin and turned to grab the tweezers from the first aid kit.

"So uh..." I cleared my throat again to stop the croaking in my voice. I began to pluck out the small pieces of glass that stuck in his skin with the tweezers. "What happened to Cole? Is he okay? Oh God, I feel like a terrible friend for leaving him there!" I was distracted by the thought of leaving him there and finally was able to take my mind off how too entirely close Ray was standing in front of me.

"No need to worry, Beauty, I told the bouncer to call an ambulance for him. We can check on him tomorrow if you want?" I nodded and breathed in relief. At least he was in good hands.

"Thank you, Ray. Okay... how's the back of your head?" I tried to twist his head so I could see but he held my wrists and brought them down.

"My head is fine. Trust me" I looked down, not being able to look into his penetrating gaze and noticed his hands still had some dried on them.

I wet another few pieces of cotton and began cleaning them, noticing that the more skin I cleared of blood the more bruising it revealed underneath. What did he do in there? Once his hands were all cleaned of blood I saw how raw and bruised his knuckles were. And it was all my fault.

My eyes teared up. I couldn't help it. I'd always faded into the background, just concentrating on getting my gym up and running, then all of a sudden I find myself the main cause of multiple men being hurt! "I'm so sorry Ray!" I squeaked lifting our entwined hands to my mouth and kissing his raw knuckles.

My tears rolled down my cheeks and landed against his knuckles as I kissed the memories and tears away with my trembling lips. "Hey, hey, hey... what's wrong? Why are you crying? What are you sorry for?" Ray sounded confused. "Baby, don't cry"

He carefully untangled our fingers and cupped my face, his eyes looking over me. I'd caused nothing but drama for Ray from the moment we met... and I was unconscious then! It was embarrassing and I couldn't understand how he'd want to be dragged into this kind of drama. I couldn't answer him... so instead he bent down and captured my bottom lip with his lips.

He sucked it into his mouth and lightly bit it as his tongue lazily swiped over the fullness. My eyes slid shut, causing another few tears to escape, and I felt one of his hands glide down my neck, my ribs and down to my lower back while his other hand cupped the back of my neck.

A moan escaped from deep within my throat and my hands had a mind of their own as they gripped the belt loops of his jeans. His tongue, lips and teeth were doing crazy things to me and it was all concentrated to my bottom lip. He hadn't tried to do more or kiss me deeper and I was practically panting with need... panting for more!

I gripped his belt loops tighter and pulled him closer to me, if that was even possible, and I bit his bottom lip back hoping he'd understand what I needed. I felt his lips curve into a smile and he pushed his tongue past my lips to stroke my own tongue. It was like fireworks inside my body were going haywire. He was driving me crazy with a simple kiss and I was close to losing my mind. What was he doing to me?!

I could feel his hardness pressing into my thigh and it made my core tighten with need. His hand pushed my lower back, making me arch into him and pressing my breasts against his bare chest. The enclosed space of the bathroom was heating up quickly. Very quickly. I couldn't get enough of him and it seemed that he felt the same way too. His hands swooped down and grabbed my ass lifting me up without any hesitation, making my legs wrap around his trim hips and pressing his engorged member against the outside of my panties.

I didn't know whether to curse my skirt or praise it!

He deepened our kiss and squeezed me tightly as he began to walk us out of the bathroom and towards my bedroom. Oh, yes! I practically moaned. He carefully laid me on the bed, crawling on top of me without ever breaking our kiss and I revelled at the feeling of lying between the soft mattress and his hard body. I felt his hand drawing circles with his thumb on my outer thigh and it slowly began tracing higher and higher until he pushed my skirt up to bundle at my waist.

He finally tore his lips away from mine and I gasped in some much needed air, which quickly turned into moaning when he nibbled down my neck and collarbone. "You are so beautiful, Seychelles" He was murmuring against my skin. I could barely hear him, though, it felt like waves were crashing in my ears but it was only my loud breathing and frantically beating heart.

His thumbs hooked into my panties and slowly dragged them down my legs, taking the time to torture me relentlessly. I wanted Ray, I needed him with a deep, burning passion. I was slightly scared at the intense emotions bursting from every pore. When he finally pulled them off he threw them away, not caring where they landed, and retraced his steps with his hands; gliding them lazily up my legs again.

"Ray!" I moaned almost painfully. It was pleasurable torture! The anticipation was almost killing me!

"Patience, Beauty" He whispered as he bit into my tube top and dragged it down as well, revealing my strapless bra. He kissed the swells of my breasts while his fingers danced along the lips of my core. "You are so wet!"

With his free hand he pulled down my strapless bra making my brea$ts push up higher as they spilled free but I barely noticed it because his fingers had inched closer and closer to my throbbing sex. His fingers found my cl!t and began rubbing around in gentle circles as he gently rolled my n!pple between his teeth. The pleasurable sensations connected between the two so fiercely I could feel the physical connection between them!

Without any warning he pushed two fingers into my core and hooked them as they began to pump in and out of me, rubbing me in just the right spot that had me screaming his name. He was sucking and biting my n!pples in turn while his hand tweaked the other and all the while thrusting his fingers in me in just the right way, at just the right speed.

I could feel my muscles tightening; feel them grabbing at him greedily for more, for deeper! "That's right baby" Ray groaned against my brea$ts, "Come for me, let it go, feel it!" His words pushed me over the edge. My back arched out of its own accord while my toes curled tightly. I screamed out all my pent up sexual tension as the most powerful orga$m erupted from inside of me and wracked my entire body with powerful convulsions.

Ray continued to slowly thrust his fingers inside of me, but once my back fell back down to the bed and my screaming ceased, he pulled his fingers out and began to suck on them, licking all my spent juices off his digits. "You taste so sweet Seychelles" He moaned.

I grabbed the back of his neck and pulled him up to kiss his lips. I could taste my essence on his lips and yet I didn't care. Ray was amazing. Purely amazing and I needed to repay him!

Chapter 18

My body was heating up and my bunched up clothes felt too hot on my skin. I pushed against Ray and immediately he rolled off. I loved that even with a simple movement he knew what I wanted. "Are you okay Seychelles?" He whispered huskily.

"You have no idea" I whispered back.

I rolled us over so that I was straddling him and chuckled when Ray's eyes widened to the size of saucers. His hands flew up to my hip bones and gripped them tightly making me jump as pleasure jolted straight to my core. Holy hell! "Touch me, Seychelles" He encouraged me.

I bit my lip and pressed my hands over his wide chest. I traced over his scars and then bent down to kiss them. With every kiss I sealed it with a lick and with every lick Ray would groan out and squeeze my hips tighter. I kissed my way up to his n!pples and nipped at them gently. The small tight buds stood erect, much like the swollen er*ction nudging my thighs.

I was more than ready to have him. I needed him!

I began to kiss my way back down his torso until I got to his jeans I popped the button out and slowly began to pull the zipper down. I looked up and saw Ray looking down, watching me with large, dark, lust-filled eyes. His breathing was ragged and his hands clenched tight, yet he didn't make a move. Ray lifted his hips as I tried to tug down his jeans and I couldn't miss the very large protrusion in his boxers while he kicked his jeans down onto the ground.

My mouth ran dry and my breathing became erratic, and I was only looking at his er*ction! Slowly I hooked my fingers into the waistband of his boxers and pulled it down letting his manhood spring out in all his throbbing glory. Ray was big, not just big but... massive. I gulped, was he going to fit in me?! A bead of moisture gathered at the tip and I was curious to how it would taste so without warning I bent down and licked it off.

Ray's hips bucked and I heard the wind escaping his lips, "Holy sh*t Seychelles!" I bit my lip trying not to smile, not letting the feeling of power over this large man over come me. I tested his length, stroking him as I brought my mouth down to swirl my tongue over the thick head of his er*ction. It throbbed in my hand and I began to stroke faster, all the while Ray's husky groans filled the silent night. "F*ck! What are you doing to me?! That feels so good!"

His moans of pleasure encouraged me and pushed me into taking him further into my mouth. All of a sudden his hands flew to my hair and tangled his fingers through the strands as he started to thrust himself gently into my mouth as well. I was dripping wet between my thighs and I closed my eyes, imagining his member imitating its strokes somewhere else besides my mouth. His length began to grow thicker and his thrusts became quicker, "Sh*t beauty, I'm going to come. You need to let go, baby...!" Ray choked out.

I could feel him begin to pull out of my mouth but I wasn't having any of that. I was inexperienced... but I knew the big deal between 'spitting or swallowing'. Instead of letting him pull out from my mouth I pushed my head down farther, squeezing his thickening member down my throat as I bobbed it quickly. I lowered my hands and cupped his sacs while continuing to deep throat him and in no time Ray let out a growl that was worthy of a battle cry. His hips bucked and my fingers tightened in my hair as his warm, thick essence spurted out of him and in my awaiting mouth. I quickly swallowed, almost gagging while I tried to swallow every drop of it.

I gently licked his semi-hard member and I felt his entire body shiver. He pulled me up next to him and kissed me. I could feel his passion in his kiss and it made me want more. Ray was amazing. He was like no one I'd ever met before and it scared me in a way to lose him. It was strange, I'd only known him for a short while and yet I felt connected to him in a way I didn't expect to ever feel towards anyone.

Ray sighed heavily and I looked up to his glowing autumn eyes. "You are amazing" He whispered, his eyes caressing my entire face. I kissed his jaw and smiled.

"You're not too bad either Lieutenant" I felt him still slightly and looked back up him, "What's wrong Ray?"

He stayed silent, almost as though he was pondering on what to say, so I gave him some time to figure out what he wanted to say while I drew circles over his sternum. I ran my finger over the smooth skin then over the flawed healed scars, wondering if he would ever tell me the stories behind them. "My physical is next month..."

The slight smile I hadn't noticed was on my lips dropped off. His physical. I don't know when it slipped from my mind that the whole reason Ray was training so hard every day was because he was training to prove he was physically able to return to the Air Force. His voice had been strained but I wasn't sure if it was because he was tired or because he was nervous about it.

I faked a smile and patted his chest, "That's great news, Ray! It's what you've been waiting and training for, right? I'm excited for you" No, I wasn't.

It was probably selfish and wrong of me to think it, but I didn't want him to go. I didn't want to say goodbye and watch his glorious back as he walked away from me... for who knows how long?! I've seen how much he loves his mom and he told me he hadn't seen her in ten years. Ten years! I wanted to explore these feelings I had for Ray and yet it seems that just when I started to get to know this gentle giant, it was already too late and he'd be leaving soon.

It was no doubt that he'd pass the test in my opinion. He was a strong man and if tonight at the club had been any consolation Ray could handle himself very well. And he'd be leaving me.

"So... you're excited for me?" He asked tentatively.

"Well yeah, you told me before that the Air Force was your dream and if anyone appreciates having their dream come true it's me with my gym. I worked hard for it to come true and now I have it, I couldn't imagine leaving it. Now there's you and your dream of being an airman and well, you've already lived it, but to have it back within your grasp so soon must feel great!"

The fake grin plastered to my face felt traitorous... but I wasn't about to ruin what we shared over the last few weeks of knowing each other because of my selfish thoughts. Ray was a brilliant man, and he deserved everything he wanted. Even if it meant I was a friend who would write to him through a letter... but then have him eventually forget about me.

Ray's POV

I gazed down at Seychelles' face, searching for any sign that she wanted me to stay. Anything at all. Instead of frowning, she was smiling at me and sounded legitimately happy for me to re-join the AF. When I found out that my physical would be next month I shoved it to the back of my mind and managed to forget it, it was easy to forget a lot of things when I was around Seychelles, but when she called me Lieutenant it all came crashing back like a hammer on a sore thumb.

Was I expecting her to ask if I wanted to stay? Maybe.

Did I want her to give me reasons to stay, her being one of them? Maybe.

Did I want to stay? I wasn't sure.

Was Seychelles a good enough reason to stay? Of course she was.

But as I searched her eyes and gazed down at her happy smile I wondered why I was even thinking like this. It was because I practically stalked her for months before she even knew me. I thought gingerly. All those early morning walks on the beach were an excuse to watch this beautiful woman beside me move her body through the water and give off a sense of freedom. I loved watching her then and I was getting frightening feelings that were telling me I could watch her like that for a long time in the future.

I shook my head. From the way she was reacting to my most probable departure I had no right to be thinking those kinds of thoughts. "Let's forget about it... I'd rather concentrate on you tonight" I winked, trying to lighten the mood from the serious turn it'd taken. I bent down and kissed her soft lips, gaining a husky moan from Seychelles and we continued to kiss as I tried to forget about the physical that would most likely rip me away from the beautiful woman in my arms.

"I should let you sleep" I whispered between kissing her eyelids. It was just after two in the morning and Seychelles was falling in and out of consciousness. We'd laid in her bed together and talked. Just talked. We talked anything and everything it seemed as though if we didn't need to sleep we could continue kissing and talking about anything for hours and hours and hours.

Seychelles moaned and cuddled closer to me. "Will I see you tomorrow?" She murmured with her eyes closed.

I slid my finger down her bare shoulder to her arm and reached down for her blanket before pulling it up to cover her still naked body. "I wouldn't have it any other way. I'd miss you too much" I smiled kissing her parted lips.

"I'd miss you too..."

I chuckled lightly to myself when she fell asleep. She seemed to like falling asleep on me. I felt a slightly painful twang in my chest at the thought of her falling asleep on some other guy. She was a gorgeous woman and, while I was surprised she was still a virgin, she was constantly surrounded by good looking men and could easily have her pick. "Goodnight" I whispered and with another kiss to her delectable lips I slipped out from between the sheets and pulled on my clothes that were scattered around the room.

The wind howled softly and I hesitated momentarily before quickly searching around the house for the cracks and holes so I could fix them easier in the daytime. Ten minutes later and I was locking Seychelles' front door behind me. The wind blew across my face and I breathed in the refreshing salt air. It brought me back to reality, something I wasn't sure I was grateful for, and hopped into car.

The drive back to my house was filled with silence. The roads were dead and the only movement was from the stay dog that seemed to roam through the streets. My house came into view and I wasn't surprised to see all the lights were out. I cut the engine and headed to the house. I entered the house and locked the door behind me before making my ay silently to my room.

The slight scent of baked goods filled the halls and I felt at home. My mom's house always smelt like baking and it made e happy that I could support my mother financially that she didn't need to work. I'd rather her do things she enjoyed than put her to work to support herself. I collapsed onto my bed and sighed. I was so confused on what to do...

Stay... Leave...

Leave... Stay...

A knock sounded on my door and I peered over to see Tom leaning against it with a grin plastered to his face. "Well... either you got lost on the way to your girlfriend's house and on the way back or the Beast came out tonight"

I stared at him and raised an eyebrow, "Where do you get half of the things you say Tom?"

He shrugged and chuckled. "I'm just talented" He looked at me properly and his grin dropped off making him look like more of the serious Tom that didn't come out very often. "What's up Beast? Looks like someone's kicked your dog"

"I don't have a dog..."

"You know what I mean"

Being the womaniser that he was I wasn't sure he was the best person to talk to but I mentally shrugged and spilled all my jumbled thoughts to him anyway. "My physical is next month... you know that. I just don't know if I want to go back"

This news barely made his eyebrows twitch. Tom thought over what I said before moving forward and sitting on the edge of my bed. "Because of Shell?" I nodded, not surprised he came to that conclusion. "You really like her then?"

My eyes darted to him before looking away, "Seems to be that way..."

"Like her, as in love her?"

I froze. I had been trying to avoid thinking about that word. Love. I'd never loved anyone in my life besides my mom and I began to feel things for Seychelles I didn't want to believe such a notion. "I don't know... I just... " I growled in frustration. It was hard talking to another man about my feelings. It was a weird feeling and made me feel vulnerable. Something I hated feeling! "Yes... Yes I love her"

I expected Tom to make some snarky comment or punch my arm and tell me to go 'bang that', but once again I was surprised when he simply nodded. "It's not hard to see you know. Even a blind man could tell you're in love with her. Look Ray... I'm not usually one to stick with one woman for very long, but I like Shell. She's a cool chick and, I don't know, I seem to get this sibling vibe with her"

"Well, she's an only child"

Tom nodded once and shrugged, "Then I'll step in and be her surrogate brother. You're my best friend Ray and I've known you a long time but think hard about what you want. Don't string Shell along, not even I do that. You need to make a choice: Tell her you love her and stay with her, or break it off and return to the AF"

I frowned, "How do you know I haven't told her I love her?"

"Because you weren't even sure of it yourself five minutes ago Bud" Tom stood up and slapped my back. "Think hard Ray. Shell's a nice chick, but I know you... If you go back to the AF you'll end up staying there like before and not returning until you're injured again. See you in the morning"

Tom closed my door behind him and I fell back against my pillows. Why the hell was Tom so observant? I closed my eyes tightly feeling the pain in my tired eyes. I was in love with Seychelles. Damn... that just made my decision even harder.

What the hell am I going to do?

I woke up to the smell of mom's waffles wafting through my door. I'd had the worst night filled with disconnected and vivid dreams of me leaving Seychelles and going back to the AF, then of me being back at the base but forgetting everything about her. I'd woken up so many times throughout the night leaving me exhausted. I'd never slept in in the months I'd been back so it was odd to wake up with other people awake.

I rubbed at my tired eyes and stalked to the kitchen to see Tom stuffing his face with mom's waffles while mom hummed softly with her back to me. "Morning" I mumbled.

My mom jumped as she turned around. "Oh Rayray! I didn't even think you were still here, usually you've already left" She walked over to me and kissed me on the cheek. "Good morning darling. I'll make you some waffles"

"I see you're taking advantage of my mom's cooking Shaw" I smirked at Tom. He chuckled and swallowed the fist sized waffled piece in his mouth.

"What can I say... It's not that hard to fall in love with your mom's cooking" He smirked back and I glowered back. I knew his serious side wouldn't last long.

"Yeah, tell me about it" My mom beamed and kissed both our cheeks making me feel as though she's practically adopted Tom as my brother.

"So planning on spending time with your mother today or going to see that gorgeous girl of yours, hmm?" My mom asked with a grin on her lips.

"I'm actually going over to her place in a bit to fix her house" Yeah... that's purely the only reason...

"Don't worry Sandy, I'll keep you company! Ray's practically ditched me anyway" I rolled my eyes at Tom. "I'll meet you at the gym later"

I knocked on Seychelles' door, suddenly nervous. Would she be able to tell that I loved her? Would it seem like it was written across my face? I wasn't sure I was read to tell her just yet... just in case my decision was to return to the AF. I knew Tom was right when he said not to string her along, and I would never do that to any woman let alone to Seychelles.

The door was wrenched open and I couldn't help the smile that crept onto my face when I looked down at Seychelles. "Good morning beautiful" I bent down to kiss her on the lips.

"Mmm, a very good morning to you too Ray" She wrapped her hands around my neck and I turned to push her against the wall as I deepened the kiss. She tasted like mint and smelled fresh from a shower and I couldn't help but instantly feel my lower half twitch in want. Damn, she was too sexy for her own good. Seychelles broke away first and laid her head against the wall with her eyes shut and a grin pulling at her lips. "I missed you"

I loved and hated the glow I felt inside at her words. It honestly wasn't helping with my decision. "I missed you too Beauty" I kissed her again softly, "I just came by to fix the house"

I pointed my thumb over at my car where it was easy to see all the materials needed to fix any cracks and holes. "Oh... I actually have a PT session this morning that I need to get to. I'm sorry, I forgot to tell you last night. You don't need to fix my place up, you know"

I could tell she was grateful and I honestly wanted her house to be totally fixed before, or if, I leave. "How about you go on ahead to your session and I'll stick around to fix everything up. By the time you're finished I should be done and then, and then I'll drive you to the hospital to see Cole"

"Oh, if you're sure Ray" She bit her lip enticingly. "Do you think he's still there?"

"Yes, I called the hospital earlier. He had to stay overnight" Seychelles nodded and stood on her toes to nip at my jaw. I felt my blood rush downwards and I cursed my inability to stop it just by her simple touches.

"You're a great man Ray Hodges... I lo- Uh... I like that shirt on you" I chuckled at her random comment but kissed her.

"Thanks beautiful... Now go on. I'll still be here when you get back" She beamed at me and hurried inside to grab her bag and slipped on her shoes before running to her car. She started the engine and blew me a kiss before driving off.

I sighed.

But would I still be here after my physical...?

Chapter 19

Sweat trickled down the length of my spine and the edges of my face as I hammered down another piece of wooden board. I knew there was a lot of work that needed to be done to shape up the house but I realised there was a lot more that needed to be done. Seychelles had mentioned it was built sometime down the generation of her family and I half wondered what in the hell they were thinking building a house mainly of wood and barely any cement to protect it from decaying.

I could understand that they wouldn't have thought this far down the line but the house was practically falling apart. I would have to talk to Seychelles about it, and ask her if she minded me doing even more work on it. A smile tugged my lips when I already knew what she should say. She'd argue with me that I didn't need to do any work, that it wasn't necessary for me to. I already knew she'd think of it as charity for her but the truth was that her safety had become a high priority for me.

All throughout the morning while I worked away I argued with myself what I was going to do: stay or leave.

A few hours later and I still haven't taken a step toward either decision! It was like a throbbing open wound. Painful and obviously needed attention but yet I was stubborn enough to try to deal with it myself. Even though it was doing no good. I'd managed to seal smaller cracks and holes while having to tear boards down completely and nailing down new ones. My body was getting a work out and for that I was thankful for. Holding back and taking it slow with Seychelles had been hard... very hard... and if it meant that having this sort of physical labour would take my mind off the way her body responded so amazingly to mine, then I'd build her a whole new damn house.

My thoughts were halted by the sound of a car coming up the driveway and after a few seconds Seychelles' car came into view. She hopped out and threw me her megawatt smile that had my heart stuttering for a few beats while she walked on over. "Wow, Ray! This looks fantastic! You really shouldn't bother with all of this you know. Please let me pay you back for-"

I swooped down and kissed her efficiently stopping her speech. "You're welcome" I whispered. "And I happen to like doing things for you Seychelles, you work so hard for everything you want and I just want to give you a little something back. Besides... I just want you safe at home"

She was biting her bottom lip and the sight of it was driving me crazy. "Thank you again, Ray. You are honest to God a dream come true" Her eyes grew big and her cheeks flushed as she stuttered and I couldn't help but laugh.

"Well, that's always nice to hear! Though it's the first time I've ever heard that about myself." I winked, which only made her face deepen to a nice scarlet. "Go on inside and freshen up and then I'll drive us to the hospital."

She nodded and walked inside leaving the front door open. "Have you had anything to drink while I was gone Ray?" she called from inside.

"No, I haven't."

Her head popped out from the doorframe with her eyes wide again. "Why not? I left the house open for you so you could've gone inside any time. Well, I'll get you a glass of water okay? Come on inside."

I was about to argue and say that I was fine. I wanted to see if there was anything that needed fixing that I could get done today but the stern look in her eyes, which looked similar to a puppy trying to look serious, made me stop and follow her inside the house. My eyes fell down to her shapely legs and pert behind and I suppressed a moan when she bent down to grab her bags from the ground. Round and ripe, perfect for biting. Her body was perfect and made me want to run my hands all over every single cell of it. Though, I was sure that no matter how she looked, and what shape she was I would want to do the same.

We walked into the kitchen after kicking off our shoes and she poured me a glass of cold water. "Here, you just relax now and I'll be quick. Make yourself at home!"

She began to walk past me but I grabbed her from around her hips and pulled her back to me so that her back was at my front. I trailed my hands up and down her hips as I softly bit her earlobes. "All that hammering and fixing was making me kind of sweaty… mind if I joined you in your shower?"

I heard her breath hitch and stop altogether before quickening and I swear the room became instantly warmer. "Uh… join me?"

"I won't push you if you don't want to, but damn Seychelle s… have you any idea how sexy you look in that little outfit of yours?" I pulled her tighter against my hardening groin and heard her gasp. "Can you feel what you do to me?"

She fell silent before turning around and facing me while I walked her back to the kitchen bench, trapping her between the bench and myself. "Okay" She whispered huskily. She stood on her toes and kissed the bottom of my chin before taking hold of my hand and leading us to her room. "I-uh… I don't know what to do…" She blushed.

"Shh… all we're doing is taking a shower"

Seychelles' POV

My heart was beating three times faster than normal and in the back of my frantic mind I wondered if that was normal, or if I should see a doctor about that. I was going to see Ray naked. Completely naked! I'd seen certain parts of naked before but this was going to be different. Were we going to make love? Was it finally going to happen?!

I breathed slowly in through my nose and exhaled quietly out my mouth. I led us into the bathroom and dropped our hands so I could turn the water on. I twisted the hot and cold knobs with trembling hands and waited for the water to warm up. Okay… now what? I turned around and gulped when I saw Ray already half way taking his shirt off. Oh wow.

All his muscles rippled with the movements and the scars on his torso danced along with it. His tanned skin held taut over said rippling muscles and I wanted to just kiss every single one.

"Need some help?" My eyes darted up to Ray to see him smirking.

"What?" I asked dumbly.

"You're looking a little lost there, Beauty. I was just wondering if you needed some help taking off those clothes"

"Honestly… I think I might" I could feel my cheeks burning. It was supposed to sound seductive, but it came out like I was suffering from some sort of brain fart and couldn't do something as simple as taking off my top. Ray didn't find it odd, however, and he smiled again showing off his prize winning dimples as he stepped forward.

"Well, then by all means, let me help you" Oh, he was so close. He smelled of sweat, apples and sea salt. Such a strange mixture, yet heady and delicious just the same. His fingers traced the bottom of my shirt and gripped it before slowly pulling it upwards. He bared my flesh bit by bit and yet his eyes never strayed from mine. It felt so intense and yet, in reality, all he's doing is removing my shirt. He pulled it over my cropped top and I held my arm above my head as he pulled it off completely.

"Need help with your leggings too?" He asked with a quirked eyebrow. I nodded helplessly.

"I may need help taking off everything, Ray" I was surprised at how husky I sounded.

Ray smiled and pressed his finger underneath my waistband so that his hands cupped my hips and he pushed his hands down, taking my leggings along with them. As he pushed them down his hands left blazing trails of heat everywhere it touched. Over my hips, over my bottom, down the back of my thighs and calves and finally my ankles and feet. He was kneeling down in front of me and surprised me by kissing his way up.

He nipped and kissed back up where his hands were and I groaned when I realised he skipped past the apex of my thighs. Once he was standing again I felt his hands tugging at the bottom of my cropped top, "You still okay with this Beauty?" His voice was deep and gruff and so sexy I wouldn't have cared if he tore the rest of my remaining clothing off!

I nodded once more and instead of pulling it off slowly like before he pulled it off quickly and his lips attacked mine. All around us the steam from the too-hot shower billowed around and clung to our bared skin. I only wore my panties and Ray still wore his jeans. I hated those jeans right now. Ray kissed me deeply and I moaned as our tongues tasted each other. His hands massaged and moulded my brea$ts, plucking at my n!pples; making me melt.

"Damn, you are so irresistible Seychelles" He murmured between kisses. "What are you doing to me?!"

I nearly cried when his hands left my chest and roamed downwards. He pulled my panties down and as soon as they were at my knees I kicked them off. I was officially naked in front of Ray, and it still didn't seem enough for me. I fumbled with the button of his jeans and pulled the zipper down.

"Careful" Ray mumbled against my lips as I pulled the zipper down over his impressive length. He kicked off the unwanted clothing and quickly disposed of his boxers.

Ray's hands grabbed the back of my thighs, just under the cleft of my buttocks and pulled me towards him; cradling me against his erection. Our moans mixed together and the heat from our bodies, the sexual atmosphere and the steam was enough to make me swoon.

Before I knew what was happening I was lifted off the ground and my legs were wrapped around Ray's waist as he walked us into the shower. The hot spray felt warm compared to my heated skin and in no time both of us were thoroughly soaked. Ray's eyes were dark and hooded and I couldn't help myself as I swooped down to capture his lips in a tongue tangling kiss. I could feel him throbbing against me and I began to tighten my legs around him, trying to get closer.

"No… no, Seychelles" Ray's voice was strained.

"What? What's wrong?"

"Only a shower" He managed to choke out.

"What?" I couldn't understand what he was talking about.

"Only a shower, Seychelles. I'm not making love to you until you're ready" He explained, yet his hips were slowly grinding against me. "Not until it's the right time"

"I'm ready now Ray. I promise, I swear! Please!" I was so wet for him, so hot for him… and it had nothing to do with the steaming shower. "Oh God, Ray, I need you!"

Ray groaned and grinded against me again. I could feel the tip of his throbbing er*ction right between my clenching thighs against the lips of my womanhood. It was so close, so close! Suddenly Ray turned us and pressed my back against the cool tiled wall, making me gasp. "Tell me what you need" He growled sexily as he lightly bit my neck.

"You" I panted.

He shook his head and spoke against my neck, "Do you need an orgasm, Seychelles?"

"Yes!" I cried straining against his strong arms to push down on his length, though it was no use. He was too strong. I squealed in surprised when he suddenly lifted me up and then tossed my legs over his shoulders; my thighs on either side of his head. "Ray!"

He breathed in deeply and tentatively licked me up with the tip of his tongue, sending waves of desire up my spine. "Well, an orgasm I can give you" Before I could tell him he misunderstood in which way I wanted said orgasm, his lips were on my cl!t and his tongue was circling around and around. My gasp was lodged halfway up my throat and I clawed at the tiled walls around me.

"Oh God, Ray!" I moaned. His hands were resting on my a$s holding me in place while his tongue trailed down to my core. He pressed it in and my eyes rolled to the back of my head. This was amazing. Ray was amazing.

"Just feel it, Seychelles" Ray groaned against me. He moved slightly and propped me in the corner of the shower while readjusting me. Suddenly he pushed in two fingers as he continued to suck on my cl!t and I couldn't stop the dam of moans that burst through past my lips. My walls were tightening and throbbing and my thighs were clenching tighter around Ray's head.

Ray moaned loudly and the vibrations pushed me over the edge. I screamed and it echoed around us yet Ray didn't stop. He circled his fingers and sucked hard on my cl!t. "No, oh God, stop! It's too much! It's too mu-!" I screamed, but it was cut short by another orgasm that wracked my entire body. My nipples strained forward and my back arched while my thighs clenched around Ray's head and even my toes were curled up tightly. I'd never had an orgasm so powerful!

Ray kissed my womanhood once more before wrapping his arms around my waist and pulling me to my feet. I moaned quietly at the feel of his stiff groin sliding down my body and revelled in the embrace Ray wrapped me in. "That was amazing Ray" I purred.

"Good. Your moaning is my favourite sound in the world" I could practically hear him grinning. I wanted to repay him. Well, I wanted more but apparently Ray wasn't having any of that, so instead I grabbed the loofah hanging from the shampoo rack and drizzled body soap over it.

"Can I wash you, Ray?" I bit my lip.

"You can do whatever you want to me, Beauty" He said huskily.

I pressed the loofah against his chest and rubbed around in circles letting the soap suds collect all over his skin. I washed his shoulders, back and down to his buttocks, all so firm and hard. I washed the backs of his legs before rounding to the front and finally reaching his throbbing manhood. I looked up at Ray and his eyes were gazing down intently on me, daring me to do anything I wanted to him.

I took up his silent dare and wrapped the loofah around his hard member, stroking up and down slowly and feeling the hard muscle behind the soft skin. His eyes closed and his hands gripped my hips tightly, but he stayed silent all except for his harsh breathing. His reaction made me confident and I quickened my stroking, going up and down before circling around the tip and repeating.

The soap suds were all washing away as the hot water cascaded down our bodies and I felt my core tighten at the sound of Ray's moan. I dropped the loofah to the ground and began to repeat the same process with my hand, loving the feel of Ray's member in my grasp. I stroked my thumb over the tip and quickly bent down to my knees as I replaced my thumb with my mouth.

Ray let out a stream of curses as I sucked hard, hollowing my cheeks, and I instantly felt his hands tangle in with my wet hair. He began to control how fast and deep I was going and the feel of being controlled like this was erotic. "Touch yourself Seychelles" Ray growled out sexily. "I can see you clenching your thighs. Touch yourself how you want me to touch you"

I didn't think twice about his instructions, no longer feeling shy or embarrassed, and purred around Ray's er*ction as my fingers circled around my core. Ray cursed again and I knew it was the sight he was getting of my lips around his member as my fingers dipped in and out of my core. Hell, I was getting turned on by the mental imagine.

"You're so sexy, Seychelles. So beautiful. Damn..." He murmured as he pumped his hips faster. My orgasm was building up and I could tell Ray was getting close too. He continued to murmur sweet nothings but I was lost in my own pleasurable world. "Sh*t, Beauty... I'm going to- You'll need to move"

I clamped my lips around his harder and pushed my head down, pushing him deeper into my throat the same time as I climaxed and I screamed around him as he moaned my name loudly and spilt his seed. "Oh sh*t! Oh sh*t! Oh sh*t!" He whispered as I gently licked him from base to tip.

Ray pulled me up and kissed me hard. "Seychelles... I don't think you realise just how deeply you've put me under your spell" He kissed my forehead and I hugged tightly, willing my mouth to stay closed.

I loved Ray.

I wanted to shout it to him. To let the world know. But I held my tongue, because telling him would cause us heart break. Even if he, by some miracle, loved me back he was still leaving. I wouldn't put myself in that heart breaking situation and I wouldn't make him choose between me and the Air Force.

The water was beginning to cool down so Ray quickly washed me, thoroughly, before shutting the water off. "Towels?" He asked.

"Over in the cupboard" I pointed at the old, white cupboard in the corner. He jumped out and grabbed two, wrapping one around his lean hips and holding the other open for me to walk into. I smiled and walked into his arms, before he patted and rubbed me dry. Just like with the soap, he was very meticulous about drying me off well.

He grabbed his boxers and jeans and slipped them on, then threw his towel in the hamper before scooping me up in his arms. I squealed in laughter, telling him to put me down. "What can I say? I like having you in my arms" He laughed back.

"Put me down! I can walk! Besides I need to get changed" He chuckled and put me to my feet.

"I'm going to grab my spare shirt from the car and wait for you in the lounge" He winked quickly slapped my behind before running out of my room.

I was on cloud nine while I changed and towel dried my hair. I threw it up in a messy bun and stared at my reflection in the mirror. My cheeks were flushed but my skin was glowing. My eyes were bright and my smile wouldn't leave my face. It looked good there... I hadn't smiled like this for a long time and ever since I met Ray I found myself smiling a lot more like this every day.

"You look good Shell" I whispered to my reflection. "You look happy"

I knew I was happy because of Ray. My smiled twitched a little at the thought of Ray leaving and I half wondered if I would still smile like this when he finally leaves. I wasn't so sure. I stood up straight and took a deep breath. I was going to enjoy this for as long as I could... and when the moment came that Ray left my life I wouldn't be sad. I would hold my head up high and remember all the good times we shared. Hopefully that included us making love... and soon.

"Alright, I'm ready!" I called out before stepping out of the room. "Let' go visit Cole".

Epilogue

I listened with a smile as Ray hummed a song I couldn't make out while he drove us to the hospital. In the space of the small car it seemed as though the vibrations from his humming was collecting directly into my lower belly. Every time I glanced at him I'd quickly look away and blush because he would so happen to be looking at me too. My body still tingled from our tryst in the shower and yet even though he'd pushed my body through multiple orgasms I couldn't help but feel that I still needed something more. His tongue and fingers were magical. Very magical. But what I wanted... what I needed, was his whole body.

On me.

In me.

I sighed quietly. Maybe I could seduce him? I almost shooed the idea away as soon as it popped in my head because my se-duction skills would be on par with my flying skills. Non-ex-istent. As we continued to drive along the road I peered up at the sky. Clouds were beginning to gather together slowly and I could already tell a massive storm would be the end result any time soon. The sun would peek from behind the clouds every once in a while and make it seem as though a giant hand was playing with the light switch and I just hoped we reached the hospital before it started raining.

We pulled into the parking lot just as it started to rain down hard. "Stay inside first, I'll get your door" Ray told me. I was about to protest and say it'd be quicker if we just ran out together but he was already slamming his door shut and running around the front of the car taking his jacket off. He threw my door open and just when I stepped out he tossed his jacket over my head and shoulders, closed my door for me before grabbing my hand and pulling us towards the building. Ever the gentleman! Even though it was only a short distance from the car to the entrance of the hospital Ray and I ended up almost soaked through by the time we stepped into the air conditioned hospital – Ray more so than I was.

"This way" Ray said tugging my hand, which he hadn't let go of, as he led us to a set of elevators. I gave him a questioning glance and he smiled, "I asked which ward he was in when I called earlier"

The elevator dinged and we stepped inside along with a frantic looking man carrying two bags and a long pillow alongside a heavily pregnant woman. "Oh God, which floor?! Which floor is it?!" The man murmured to himself. Ray stepped forward and pressed the fourth floor button as well as the seventh, throwing a look at the woman who was currently concentrating extremely hard on her breathing and ignoring her partner completely.

"I'm going to take a stab in the dark and say you're looking for the labour ward?" Ray drawled out. The man nodded.

"Yeah... I happened to see the sign outside. Yours is the fourth-"

He was interrupted by the woman making some sort of grunting and whining sound and I stood in my spot unsure what to do. This situation was beyond awkward. The elevator dinged again and Ray nodded at the opening doors. "Good luck" I offered bleakly as the woman's face relaxed and she grinned.

"Thanks... I swear my husband will need the drugs more than I do" She rolled her eyes before walking out with her husband trailing after her. The doors shut again and once we were moving along Ray and my eyes connected and we burst out laughing.

"Well that was unexpected!" I giggled. Ray laughed loudly beside me.

"If that was me and you I'd probably be the same as the husband" He laughed. My smile dropped from my face as I considered his words. Was that a hint that he saw some sort of future with me? Or was I completely looking too much into nothing?

The elevator stopped twice more before we reached the seventh floor and Ray grabbed my hand again before leading the way down the hall to the nurses desk. I somewhat recall him asking the nurse which room was Cole's but I couldn't concentrate on him talking when all my attention was focused on his fingers tangling themselves between mine. I mean, I was new at all this lovey dovey stuff, but I know that this was more of an intimate hand holding than normal.

It's nothing, Seychelles! He probably doesn't even realise he's doing it... I scolded myself. Ray thanked the nurse and we were off again. Finally we turned into a large open room with four beds, one in each corner of the room, with curtains drawn around two of them. Cole was sitting in the far right side, reading a magazine, when we walked up to him. Immediately I jumped to him and hugged him tight.

"I'm so sorry Cole!" I squeaked. I knew Cole had been beaten down by the guys in the club, but I had no idea how extensive they had been about it. Cole's right eye had completely swelled shut and was sporting all the different hues of black, blue and purple while his nose had several cuts and stitches across it. He didn't wear a shirt and instead was wearing thick bandages around his midsection. "Geez, are you okay?"

"I'm fine, I'm fine, Shell. Don't worry. It would've been seven shades worse if it wasn't for Ray. I never did get to thank you for that man" Cole grimaced while offering his hand. Ray nodded and shook his extended hand.

"No need to thank me, I should be thanking you for putting yourself between those pricks and Seychelles. At least I got the pleasure of whooping their asses" Ray smirked.

"Well if I wasn't too busy swallowing my own blood then I would've gotten a few punches in, I'm sure" Cole joked.

Ray sat in the spare chair in the corner and dragged me to fall into his lap. I didn't fail to notice that he made every conscious effort to always touch me somehow , whether it was holding my hand, stroking my hip, tracing his fingertips up my arm or even a hidden kiss at the back of my neck.

It was driving me mad and I wasn't even sure he knew the effect it was having on me. My panties were beyond soaked, both from rain and his heated touches and fleeting kisses, goosebumps ran all up my exposed skin and I was practically gnawing through my bottom lip!

"So uh... when are you allowed out?" I asked distractedly.

"Right about now" We all turned to a greying nurse and saw her briskly walk up to Cole. "So all your paperwork has been through and the Doc is happy with the results, so you're free to go. If you have any consistent or worsening headaches I want you to come back immediately okay?"

Cole nodded and she threw us a smile before power walking down to another patient. Well, looks like I'm a free man now! Thank God... the only reading material within my reach was this pregnancy magazine... I'm not so sure whether I want to forgo having kids now, or go visit my mom with every intention of renaming her Superwoman!"

Ray and I exchanged amused looks and both burst out laughing.

I waved as Cole shut the door to his house and sat back down properly while Ray came back from helping Cole get into his place. The rain was still pounding down heavily and I shivered slightly considering I was still wet. "Poor guy... he got soaked. Oh well..." Ray murmured as he shook out his growing hair.

"It doesn't look like this weather is going to let up anytime soon. What a shame, it started off as such a nice day too" I commented.

"Perfect for movies on the sofa and take out? Tonight?" Ray smiled tilting his head a little to the side, giving him the impression of a puppy dog.

I leaned forward across the car and kissed him gently on the side of his chin, going upwards until I reached his ear and whispered, "Sounds like a date to me"

Ray growled softly and just as he turned to kiss me I pulled back and giggled. "Save it for later stud. Now drive!"

He laughed and bowed his head before driving down the street towards my house. Ray was a huge distraction. He made me laugh without trying, smile without even knowing and took up every inch of space in my mind without having to be in the same room. I desperately needed to finish off some paperwork for my clients and the new members of the gym, that I told Ray to go spend some time with his friend while I finished them off at home. I honestly hated having to say it, because something in the back of my head told me I could spend every waking (and sleeping) moment with him, but it was practically impossible to do anything work related with Ray anywhere near me.

"Are you sure?" Ray asked seriously as we stood in my front door.

"Yes. I have a lot of work to finish and you need to spend some time with Tom. God knows how much he's driving your mother crazy" I joked. "Besides, I'm seeing you tonight anyway right?"

Ray bent down while lifting my chin up and gently bit my lower lip. His teeth gently rolled my bottom lip between them and he sucked it into his mouth before sucking on it again only to release it a few seconds later. "You couldn't keep me away from you even if you tried, Beauty"

If he wasn't holding my chin, I was positive that I'd be a puddle of melted emotions right on the doorway.

"See you later beautiful" He whispered with another peck to my lips.

"Bye" I squeaked.

I watched Ray run quickly back to his car as the rain pelted against him and once he was inside I blew him a kiss. He motioned for me to go inside and I knew he wouldn't leave until I was safely in my house, so I sent him a smile and closed the door. Leaning against the wooden door I sighed wistfully and slid down to the ground.

"I am way over my head"

Ray's POV

The familiar smell of baking goods wafted to my nose the moment I stepped into my house. I followed the sounds of Tom and my mom into the kitchen and laughed at the sight I found. Instead of the usual scene of Tom sitting on the counter as he stuffed his face with cookies and my mom doing the baking, I found my mom sitting by the bench leaning over as she threw instructions to my best friend. Tom was wearing my mom's floral apron hooked around his neck and tied behind his back as he balanced three hot trays of muffins between his floral oven gloves.

"Wow, Shaw... one day with my mom and you've officially lost it!" I laughed loudly, "What the hell are you wearing?!"

At the sound of my entrance the two looked at me, Tom dropping the trays onto the bench first, and laughing along with me. "What?! You don't like it? I think the multitude of flowers match my eyes perfectly Beast" Tom preened as he posed in his floral apron and mittens.

I quickly took a snap shot on my phone and saved it. "You just wait til the boys back at the base see this" I guffawed.

"I think he looks fine, Rayray. Don't tease him" My mom scolded me even though she was smiling brightly.

"Yeah, man! Besides, the boys wouldn't even find this strange for me" Tom threw at me. I nodded, giving in, he had me there. Tom was a unique character and didn't seem to have it in him to ever be embarrassed. So it didn't surprise me that he didn't care about me showing off his more feminine side to the other airmen.

"You're back early. I half suspected you'd stay out all day with Shell" Mom said after kissing my cheek.

"She has some paperwork to do so I'm seeing her later" I shrugged, "Guess you probably regret coming over here then huh Tom"

Tom was already stuffing his face with muffins and huffing at the same time considering they would've still been scorching hot. "Pfft, I think not! Do you even realise how good a cook and baker your mom is?! If you don't visit her more often I will take your place and she can adopt me and feed me all her delicious food. For shame Beast!"

I rolled my eyes but my mom seemed to love having a constant flirt and compliment machine around the house, "Oh Tommy you're too sweet!" She gushed.

The rest of the day I listened in to my mom and Tom's chit chat as I massaged my thigh. The rain and the cold had gotten to it again and it was starting to feel a little stiff. I wondered if the ache would ever go away or if I was always going to feel the mementos of the bullets in my leg. I was leaning towards the latter.

This brought me back to my big decision.

I would never be back to my one hundred percent again as I had been before. I'd gone through being shot before but not to this extent. Maybe it was a good a time as ever to retire while I was on top of my game and not retire when I was packed up in a wooden box with a flag draped over me. Then again, it was easily something I could work with. It didn't matter that it felt a little stiff when it got cold and wet, I would be physically active most of the time and busy if I went back. I wouldn't be looking for things to do and relaxing all the time.

Pros and cons. Pros and cons.

With every pro I came up with, there was a con. As girly as I was beginning to sound even to myself, it felt as though my head wanted one thing while my heart said another. I shook my head and concentrated on trying to mimic Seychelles' movements when she massaged my leg. Thoughts of her had me glancing over at the clock and mentally counting that I still had a few more hours until I was to drive over and have our lazy date night in.

"Want some?"

I looked over at Tom and saw him offering me a muffin. I eyed it carefully. "Uh... I don't think so. I think I might pass on it" Tom rolled his eyes and continued to gorge himself. "I'm going to take a bath, my leg is killing me"

Armed with an umbrella this time, I jumped out of the car and walked up to Seychelles front door. I knocked firmly on the door and felt a little adolescent at the wait to see her. The door swung open and I nearly swallowed my tongue. "Damn, you're a beautiful sight"

Seychelles' face turned scarlet and as she cast her eyes down in embarrassment. She wore a large baggy, knitted sweater over tiny shorts and stood barefoot in the door frame. "Oh shush, you" She blushed, "Come on inside"

I grinned and set the umbrella just outside the door and followed her inside before shutting the door behind me. The first thing I noticed was that it was slightly warmer and no rain dripped through the ceiling. I felt proud knowing it was my hard work that was able to help Seychelles live a little more comfortably. Even if it was to stop wind from creeping inside and deter the rain to run into the gutters instead of inside the roof.

Seychelles turned around I held the plastic bag of Chinese food up along with the small ten dollar bouquet of assorted flowers I decided to buy as well. Her smile dropped from her face and a look of awe took over. "Thank you so much Ray" She whispered, taking the flowers from me. "They're beautiful and so thoughtful! And thank you for fixing up the house, too"

I shrugged and placed the take out on the coffee table before bundling her to my chest. "I missed you" I murmured. "To be honest, I've never felt this emotional about someone before. What is it about you that has me racing out the door to see more of you?"

I kissed her and pressed my hand on her lower back so her flattened against me, but the contact didn't last long. I pulled her to the sofa and noticed she already had a movie lined up and waiting to be watched. Seychelles had picked a comedy to watch and we laughed and mimicked the actors all through our dinner. I found myself watching her and every little thing she did, I learned that she loved to shout at the television and picked out the capsicums from her food, and other small things. When we were finished we sat side by side on the sofa and she leaned her head against my arm, her eyelashes tickling me every blink. "I haven't felt this warm inside my own house in the rain for a while, and I have you to thank"

"You're welcome" I smiled. I was about to say that I'd do anything for her, but considering my big decision I was stuck on, I held my tongue. "I actually needed to talk to you about that. I noticed this morning that your place actually needed more fixing. The beams and framework need some fixing or changing and just more general up keeping. It looks like it's been a while since anyone's had a look at the structure of it"

"Oh yeah, I've just been so busy that I've never had the time to book someone to come along, let alone pay for it to be done"

"I'll do it for free" I shrugged.

"No Ray. Please, you've done way too much already I couldn't possibly let you do this for free!"

I leaned in closer with a smirk on my lips, "Okay... I'll take payment with kisses" And I leaned down to capture her lips with mine. "With kisses like these, I may have to charge you extra".